"Why do you do that?" Kelly asked softly.

"What, Kelly?" His finger traced the tender curve of her lips.

"Why do you slick your hair back when it's wet?" Her breath was warm against his cool skin, as their eyes met and held.

"If I didn't, it would fall into curls all over my head." He traced the smooth, straight edge of her teeth. "Not a very masculine thing, is it?"

"But it would be beautiful." Kelly's breath was coming in short, quick gasps.

"Beautiful?" He laughed, intent on exploring her sensual lower lip.

"Yes, beautiful," she insisted stubbornly, "and don't say it wouldn't be masculine. Nothing could make you less . . . less—"

"Would it make you happy if I let it curl, sweetheart?" Jake asked, chuckling softly as the color bloomed again in her cheeks.

"Yes, it would," she answered softly.

"Then why don't you fix it?"

"What?" Surprise shook her voice.

"Touch me, Kelly. Run your fingers through my hair. Touch me as I'm touching you. . . ."

WHAT ARE *LOVESWEPT* ROMANCES?

They are stories of true romance and touching emotion. We believe those two very important ingredients are constants in our highly sensual and very believable stories in the *LOVESWEPT* line. Our goal is to give you, the reader, stories of consistently high quality that may sometimes make you laugh, sometimes make you cry, but are always fresh and creative and contain many delightful surprises within their pages.

Most romance fans read an enormous number of books. Those they truly love, they keep. Others may be traded with friends and soon forgotten. We hope that each *LOVESWEPT* romance will be a treasure—a "keeper." We will always try to publish

LOVE STORIES YOU'LL NEVER FORGET
BY AUTHORS YOU'LL ALWAYS REMEMBER

The Editors

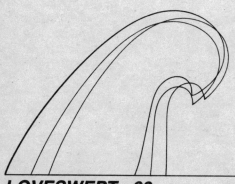

LOVESWEPT • 60

BJ James
When You Speak Love

BANTAM BOOKS · TORONTO · NEW YORK · LONDON · SYDNEY · AUCKLAND

WHEN YOU SPEAK LOVE
A Bantam Book / September 1984

ISBN 0-553-21666-X

Published simultaneously in the United States and Canada

Bantam Books are published by Bantam Books, Inc. Its
trademark, consisting of the words "Bantam Books" and
the portrayal of a rooster, is Registered in U.S. Patent and
Trademark Office and in other countries. Marca Registrada.
Bantam Books, Inc., 666 Fifth Avenue, New York, New
York 10103.

PRINTED IN THE UNITED STATES OF AMERICA

O   0 9 8 7 6 5 4 3 2

For those who have been patient,
and especially
for she who counts footsteps.

Prologue

The sleek, low lying Porsche hurtled through the deepening night. Hugging sharp curves, its solid chassis hardly swayed as the car ate up the miles. It was at its best at this speed and on these winding roads, a blue bolt of mechanical perfection that streaked toward the horizon as the last ribbon of twilight faded from the sky. Its headlights sparkled and glistened over the pavement, wet from a misty rain, then flashed crazily across pasture fences and tall pines. Again and again, the driver accelerated through one hairpin curve after another. Faster and faster, gathering momentum, the car became a shadowy blur in the velvet night.

"Slow down, you fool!" the driver of a black Seville said through tightly clenched teeth. He was following the Porsche at a saner pace, never taking his eyes from the taillights that were rapidly growing smaller in the distance.

The Seville, in its own way, could corner and hug curves, but not as well as the thundering machine ahead. This driver, with a cooler head, drove cautiously, relying on consistent performance rather than spurts of speed and daring.

It was not the Porsche that failed. Human error and faulty judgment took precedence over precise performance. A too sharp curve, the insane speed, and the rain-slick road combined to become the final catalyst.

"Oh God! No!" In unspeakable horror, the driver of the Seville watched helplessly as the blue car failed to negotiate a curve and took flight into the emptiness of a starless sky.

The Porsche hit the rocky hillside with devastating force. Crashing into an outcropping of massive stone, the car poised there, teetered for a fleeting second, then tumbled end over end. It became a lethal projectile, clipping trees and small bushes, flattening the briers and brambles in its path.

Metal scraped across granite in an agonizing shriek. Had there been one to hear, the sound would have been unbearable. One final roll and the now shapeless mass came to rest, right side up, against a tall and stately pine.

There was silence except for the sound of gasoline pouring from the ruptured tank, the overpowering odor of the deadly fuel permeating the air. The pool grew, moving in an ever widening circle, then trickled toward a wisp of smoke that was drifting in the light breeze. Small fires were beginning to blaze across the parched hillside. The shower of sparks caused by the friction of metal against rock had fed on summer dried grass and become flaming tongues. There was no sound from within the car. Nothing intruded on the stillness but the steady drip, drip of the gasoline and now the ominous crackle of fire. It was only a matter of minutes before the greedy flames would find the river of gasoline. Then nothing would stop the fire as it raced along the path, its ultimate goal the tortured, twisted ruin that had once been a work of art and power.

The sharp report of a slammed car door broke into the island of quiet. A tall, broad figure appeared at the top of the embankment, then stared in anguish at the scene below.

"God help me!" Without a moment's hesitation, he launched himself down the steep slope. Briers tore at his clothing and lashed at his skin, embedding themselves in his flesh. As he gathered speed, stones were dislodged beneath his feet and tumbled about him.

He raced the flames that moved relentlessly

toward the Porsche. With an uncanny agility he plummeted downward, never stumbling nor falling. The flames had just begun to feed upon the brambles by the car when he reached it in a final leap. He had not won the race, but neither had he lost.

Mindless of the pain, he reached through the fire for the door handle. The skin of his fingers was seared and stuck on the twisted metal. He pulled desperately, but the door, which was crumpled like a giant accordion, would not open. He looked about him for a stick, a stone, anything to serve as a wedge. There was nothing. To buy time, he used his elegantly shod feet and bare hands to stamp out the flames that were creeping closer to the spilled gasoline and the partially filled fuel tank.

Satisfied that he had held back the deadly tide, he smashed out the remaining glass from the windshield with his hands. It was difficult to reach the body sprawled on what had once been a white leather seat, and his muscles strained and twisted as he maneuvered to reach the limp form. An errant shard of glass cut a deep furrow across his ribs as he backed slowly from the gaping hole, gently bringing the driver with him.

Sparing no thought to his own blistered and bleeding hands, he gathered the once handsome man closer in his arms and, with surprising speed, moved away from the growing fire. He carried his burden for a great distance, then carefully lowered him to the ground.

Intent on his inspection of the injured man, he was not aware when the flames at last reached their destination. With a sudden and strangely muted explosion that sucked all the oxygen from the surrounding area, the blue Porsche became an inferno. The flames leaped higher and higher, black smoke and the stench of burning rubber heavy in the air.

Cautiously and with loving hands, he soothed the battered body, knowing the injuries were beyond his scope. Gently positioning the twisted, broken legs he wiped the blood from the mutilated mouth, then started back up the hillside to seek help. At his first step he was stopped in midstride by a sound that turned his blood to ice.

"Jake?" It was a tortured moan, little more than a whisper and hardly human.

"Jake! Jake! Where are you? I can't see you!" Pain and fear blended into hysteria as the injured man struggled to rise.

In one quick stride, he was back by his side. "I'm here," he said quietly. "You're badly hurt. I have to get help."

"No!" A bloody hand clutched at his shirt sleeve. "Don't leave me."

"I have to. I won't be gone long, I promise." He carefully loosened the hand and stood up again.

"Please . . . no. Don't leave me in the dark. Please . . ." The voice trailed away, then with the strength of an anguished need, rose again in a ragged breath. "Jake!"

"I'm here."

"Cold . . . so cold . . ."

In an instant the man was back on his knees, gathering the slight body in his arms. With his own warmth he tried vainly to stem the chill that was spreading as life flickered and faded, slowly but inexorably.

For a long while there was only the labored breathing of the man in his arms. Compassion and impotent rage battled within Jake's heart.

"Jake?"

"Shhh, don't talk. Save your strength."

"There's no need. I've really done it this time." A hoarse chuckle began deep in his chest, only to be cut off by a spasm of pain. With patience he waited for it to pass, his body convulsed against the onslaught. Gradually the wave crested and ebbed. He relaxed as his breathing steadied, but only slightly.

"Dying's not so bad." The weak voice faltered. He licked his lips and gathered the remnants of his fading strength. "Except . . . except Kelly. You'll take care of Lydia, but Kelly—Oh, God!" Pain of emotional anguish contorted his features. His bloody fingers gripped Jake's shirt surprisingly strong. His glazed eyes rolled back and the lids fluttered as he valiantly fought to remain conscious.

"Don't talk anymore," Jake said urgently. "Just hang on. Surely someone has seen the smoke. Someone will come. We'll get you some help. *Hang on!*" His strong arms tenderly cradled the battered body.

"Must talk . . . have to tell . . . must . . ." The ragged breathing halted as another spasm contorted the bloodless lips.

"Jake!" Panic gave an added power to the fading voice. "I can't see you. Where are you?"

"I'm here. I'll always be here."

"Go to her. I owe her so much. Find her. Tell her . . . ask her to forgive me. Please, help me . . . one last time . . . Help Kelly."

"Shhh." Jake smoothed back the light brown hair. "I'll find her."

"Promise." The word was little more than a sigh. The clutching hand relaxed and fell away, leaving a bloody trail across the white shirt. His head dropped to his chest as his eyes finally closed.

The wail of a distant siren pierced the misty air. In minutes there were voices and bright lights on the roadside above. Jake was unaware of the frenzied activity. His face, illuminated by the flickering of the burning car, was etched in sorrow.

"Would you look at that, raining and still the grass is burning," a young voice exclaimed.

"Takes more than a little shower to keep grass this dry from burning," a deeper and older voice replied. "All the sprinkle of rain did was make the road slick."

"Come on," said the younger. "We'd better go down."

The paramedics found Jake sitting utterly still. He was holding the lifeless body close to his own, whispering his promising over and over again.

"It's all right, mister. You can let him go now. We'll take care of him."

"God! Would you look at his hands!"

"Mister?"

Jake didn't respond. He didn't know anyone else was there as his mind denied all that had happened.

"Easy now." Gentle hands unlocked the burned fingers. "It's okay. We'll take good care of him."

Reluctantly, Jake allowed the ambulance attendant to take his brother from his arms. Voices, low and professional, drifted back to him.

"There's nothing we can do for this one."

"No. Better see to the other guy. His hands are a mess."

"Sir? Can you come with us? We'll have you fixed up in no time."

With gentle care not to touch the man's injured hands, the paramedic carefully helped Jake to his feet. All the way up Jake's empty gaze never left the sheet covered stretcher ahead.

One

As the final notes of her last song for the evening faded away, Kelly slid her tired fingers from the keyboard. She sat motionless as the chatter that had been cautiously muted while she played, swelled and reverberated through the room. Lost in a sea of sound, she poised there, too exhausted even to arch her back and ease the strain.

For hours she had played virtually nonstop, answering requests, laughing and talking, smiling at the customers' jokes. It was not uncommon for men and women to linger at the piano, sharing a moment with the woman of the golden hair and ready smile. Her face, calm and serene despite its flashing dimples, inspired confidence. Nightly, an uncounted number of troubled patrons left her piano with a lighter step.

The regular customer, one who had been coming to this bar for months or even years, knew that Kelly O'Brian had troubles of her own. They knew only by observation, and by the visible changes in her life. She had never been heard to complain, nor had she ever asked for help. Night after night she was here at her piano, a friendly smile on her lips, her softly curling hair turning to sunshine beneath the lights.

Now Kelly wasn't smiling, as she stared at her trembling hands. Although she willed herself not to, she lifted her head slowly to look at the man who had stared unwaveringly at her all evening.

She was calmer this time. She realized he was a stranger, someone only passing through. Yet earlier, for a moment, she had thought he was Scott. When their eyes had met, a searing pain of recognition had knifed through her. But now she could see he was taller, broader, his skin darker, his eyes colder.

His was an assessing and coldly calculating look as though he regarded her as an object, not a person. Perhaps an object of questionable value? She shuddered beneath the intense scrutiny and looked away, unable to challenge the penetrating blue stare.

Kelly would have been aware of him in spite of his resemblance to Scott or his disconcerting stare. Nick's Piano Bar and Grill was a typical neighborhood bar. It had small tables covered with checkered tablecloths, candles in wax covered wine bottles, and a sign at the door that boasted of live nightly entertainment. It was a pleasant place but not one suited to this man's elegance.

He was too well dressed in a charcoal gray suit. Its cost, Kelly thought ruefully, would pay her rent for months. Its crisp, clean lines emphasized his leanly muscled body, and even in the smoky light he looked fit and tan. His soft brown hair, burnished with streaks of gold, was neatly trimmed but seemed at odds with his sleek, suave image. It curled. Probably, she thought as a small smile played across her lips, it curled in defiance of all his efforts to the contrary.

He looked like a man with command and assurance. From the patrician nose, the chiseled jaw, and the determined set of his broad shoulders, one knew with a certainty he would always be in control. Of everything, that is, but his crisply curling hair. In her nervous state, Kelly almost giggled aloud, for even now a wayward lock fell over his forehead.

She knew she was mistaken but he seemed oddly, hauntingly like Scott. How could a man of such obvious wealth and power remind her of poor, weak Scott? No. There was nothing of Scott in this man. And yet . . . No! Kelly buried the thought deeply in her mind.

Against her will, her eyes strayed to him again, and she wondered why he was here. Why this part of town? Why this particular bar? It was not his kind of place. He wasn't a man who would enjoy slumming. Kelly drew herself up short, amazed at her own thoughts. How could she presume to know what sort of man he was by the cut of his clothes or the arrogant tilt of his chin!

"Careful, girl," she muttered to herself. "Soon you'll be needing your own 'piano psychology.' "

"Kelly?"

She looked up to see Nick standing by her side. There was worry in his kind brown eyes as he rested his hand lightly on her shoulder.

"You look tired tonight." His voice was concerned. "Want me to call you a cab?"

"Thanks, Nick, but you know I need the exercise. I'll walk." She flashed him a smile, the dimple deepening in her cheek, and patted his hand.

"Sure?"

"I'm sure, Nick."

With a quick squeeze of her shoulder, he acknowledged his defeat and walked away. Kelly sighed as she watched him weave through the tables, greeting his customers by name, most of whom were old friends and neighbors.

Nick had been her salvation. Without this small, quick-witted man what would have become of her? He had given her back her old job and with it a measure of her self-esteem. He had assured her that the job was hers for as long as she was able to handle it.

Could she hold out another nine weeks? She had to; she would need every penny. If she were frugal, perhaps she would manage. Nick no doubt suspected it was the fare rather than the need for exercise that kept her from taking a cab home. He would gladly have paid the fare, but in his kindness he'd never have offered. She knew he was sensitive about helping her keep the little pride she had left intact.

Jake Caldwell had been nursing the same drink for the better part of an hour. All evening he had been oblivious to the laughter and conversation around him. His attention had been riveted on the woman at the piano. The billboard at the door proclaimed that she was Kelly O'Brian, appearing nightly, and performing songs and requests. She was not especially talented, but played with flair and a style uniquely her own. He had watched and listened as she quieted the bar with her melodic love songs, then made the people smile and tap their toes with her gay, upbeat numbers.

He had watched her slender shoulders and arms move gracefully as her fingers drifted over the keyboard. She looked absurdly small when viewed across the highly lacquered expanse of the ancient baby grand, whose darkness mirrored her tawny appeal. She was not beautiful, yet when her golden head bent low, tilting regally, the light that played across her face gave it a poignant sweetness. And when she smiled, a man could forget to breathe as he lost himself in the radiance.

Her surroundings were right, he thought as he gazed about the room disparagingly, but still she was not the usual type. Her quiet serenity and elegant grace were a drastic departure from the blatant voluptuousness of the women Scott usually had chosen.

Jake frowned as his thoughts turned to the misguided life of his brother. At thirty-two, Jake had spent a good part of his life rescuing Scott from one woman after another, and there had been times when the woman had been the victim. With his boyish good looks and a nonchalant charm enhanced by great wealth, Scott had learned early the power he wielded over women. He had loved them all, from the simple innocent to the calculating sophisticate, but he had loved them with a fickle heart.

Two years ago, Jake had reached his limit. He had finally grown sick of Scott's escapades and had sworn never to become involved again. Yet here he sat in a neighborhood bar, staring at a mysterious woman called Kelly.

Throughout the evening he had absorbed the atmosphere of the place, his keen eyes missing nothing, and still his questions remained unanswered.

The attitude of the customers puzzled him. The woman was not beautiful, lacking the plastic perfection of most entertainers, but neither was she unattractive. Yet not once had he seen the overt familiarity a woman in her profession often faced. In its stead was a gentle, protective affection.

She was an enigma. For hours she had played, laughed, even shared jokes with an infectious gaiety, then without warning the sparkle had been snuffed out. She sat quietly now at the silent piano while Jake waited, watching, never taking his eyes from her.

Kelly stirred, reluctantly forcing herself to move. She closed the piano and rose heavily from the bench. With a wan smile, she waved in answer to a called good night. As she stepped from behind the piano her dress caught, pulling tautly across her body. A stifled gasp shattered the momentary hush that had fallen over the room.

Kelly stiffened in surprise. She was among friends here, people who had known her for most of her life. She had forgotten how a newcomer might react to her condition. Careful not to look his way, she straightened her shoulders and walked slowly, but with dignity, through the room.

At the door, she shrugged into her worn yet serviceable black coat, worrying how much longer she could wear it. Then she forgot everything as the crippling fatigue she had fought all evening gripped her with a vengeance. It weighed her down making every movement a supreme effort. She had grown accustomed to being perpetually tired and had learned to cope with it. But tonight she felt even worse. Was this the turning point? Had she reached her limit? What then could she do?

"Oh, God! I won't think about it, not tonight," she murmured to herself. She turned to the door, moving on leaden feet. At the moment she wanted nothing more than to get home, lie down, rest, and hopefully sleep.

Jake's piercing blue gaze had followed her as a

black scowl formed on his face and a strange, aching pain curled in his chest. From the first he had found this to be a puzzling situation. None of the usual rules seemed to apply. Jake had not known what he might find, but never in his wildest speculations had he expected this.

She was pregnant, her body swollen with the first, slight distortions. Pregnant, but not with Scott's child. Her small size attested that she was in the first trimester, and Scott had been home for months. A sad bitterness welled within him. Perhaps she had been the usual type after all. She had obviously wasted no time in finding another man. But a lover or a husband?

Her condition in itself should have released Jake from his promise. Instead he kept remembering a brother who had been more courageous in dying than in living. He heard again the plea for help, one last time.

Jake finished his watery drink, his eyes bleak as in his memory he relived the senseless accident that had taken Scott's life. He stared at the hand, but did not see the scars left by shattered glass and fire. He was no longer in Nick's Bar and Grill but on a steep hillside, holding a lifeless body, promising to find a woman called Kelly.

Even as he recovered from the painful wounds, Jake had set into motion the search for the woman. His only clue had been a blurred snapshot found among Scott's papers. There had been no address, no other information, only the name Kelly O'Brian scrawled across the back. It had been sheer, blind luck that the investigator had recognized a landmark in the background. After long weeks of searching Atlanta, Jake had found her.

He wanted to walk away. He wanted to forget he had ever heard the name Kelly O'Brian. But he had promised. Angrily, he slid back his chair and sauntered over to the bar. As Nick took his order for a fresh drink, Jake casually broached the subject.

"Your piano player seems familiar," he said, "but

I can't place her. Has she played here long?" He reached for the drink and leaned negligently on the bar, but the tense curve of his mouth belied his casualness.

"She's worked here off and on for years, but only for about five months this time. She's never played anywhere else, only here."

"How long will she stay this time?"

"Until the baby comes, if she can," Nick said quietly.

"And what does her husband say about that? Or is there one?" Jake's smile didn't reach the ice blue of his eyes.

"No!" Nick turned abruptly, signaling that this part of the conversation was off limits.

"Doesn't she have any family?" Jake persisted, his voice soft as he frowned with concern. He was irritated with himself. Why should he care? The woman was obviously another of Scott's tramps. One who passed from one man to the next in rapid succession. She might look like an angel, but her body didn't lie.

"There's no family that I know of," Nick said. "The kid was raised by an elderly aunt. Worked her way through college playing piano right here, taught school for a year, then gave up her job when she got pregnant." Nick stopped short. "Say! What is this? What's it to you? She's a good kid, down on her luck, and to top it off she's seven months pregnant. She can't take any more hassles, not from anybody!"

"There'll be no hassle, I assure you," Jake said smoothly. "I know a friend of hers. I'm here to help, if she'll let me." He tossed some bills on the bar and strode toward the door, pausing only once to glance at the silent piano before he stepped out into the night.

He breathed deeply of the crisp mid-October air, glad to be away from the smoke filled bar. He hated bars, and at this moment he hated himself and Kelly O'Brian and, God forgive him, he hated Scott most of all.

He crossed the street and slid behind the wheel of

his sleek black Seville. He didn't start the engine immediately, but sat clutching the steering wheel, staring into the darkness. As garish neon signs blinked off and on, Nick's words pounded through his head in an endless refrain. Seven months . . . seven months. It fit. A sudden black rage swept over him and he smashed his fist against the wheel.

"Damn you, Scott! What have you done this time?"

Kelly walked the six blocks slowly, growing more tired with each step. Had she been alone, she would have found the darkened streets frightening. But tonight she had her usual companion, Mike Cannon, the beat cop. He strolled along by her side, shortening his long stride to match hers. She smiled to herself as she thought of how Mike was always patrolling this particular part of his beat at precisely the time she walked home each night.

He was a big, bluff man, old enough to be her father. If she had expressed her gratitude, he would have blustered and denied his kindness. So she held her peace, thankful for the warmth and security he offered.

Tonight, though, she was in his company in body alone. Her mind turned again and again to the cold eyes that had watched her across that smoky room.

"You're quiet tonight, Kelly," Mike said in his deep, rumbling voice. "Is something wrong?"

"No." She shrugged. "Just thinking."

"Truth?"

"Scout's honor." She grinned up at him. "I really am fine, Mike. I wish you wouldn't worry so much about me."

"Somebody has to," he growled.

"How are Kathleen and the boys?"

Mike smiled, obviously not fooled for a minute that she was diverting his attention from herself to his favorite subject. "They're great. Got a letter from Joey last week. Looks like he might make the dean's list this semester."

"Mike! That's terrific! Next time you write to him, tell him I said hello." Kelly had grown up in the neighborhood. Only a few years older than Mike's boys, she had known all of them.

"He asked about you. You were always his favorite."

They walked in companionable silence for a block. At every step, Mike seemed to have to slow his pace as Kelly grew increasingly tired.

"Kelly?"

"Hmmm?"

"Have you heard from him?" He spat the last word as if it were poison.

"Don't, Mike. Please don't," Kelly whispered through trembling lips. "He's gone. I won't hear from him, ever."

"But, dammit, he owes you. He . . ." Mike sputtered to a stop as she raised her head to look at him. Her eyes were shimmering with unshed tears.

"I wouldn't want to keep him if he didn't want to stay. Not even for the baby's sake. No, Mike," she said gently. "An unwilling father would be worse than no father."

"I suppose that's true," he admitted grudgingly, the doubt strong in his words.

"I know it is."

"All right, Kelly." His voice grew soft but insistent. "What you say about him is true, but you're going to need help from someone. You can't do this alone."

"Yes, I can," she said firmly. "I can make it. I always have." Her resolve grew with each word.

"You have, haven't you?" Admiration for her spirit glowed in his eyes. "Just remember, though, Kathleen and I are always here if you need us."

"I know that." One tear escaped to trickle down her face. "You'll never know how much it means to know that *somebody* cares."

She continued walking, but Mike stopped her with a gentle hand on her arm. Kelly looked up, surprised to see they were standing at the entrance of her apartment building. Impulsively, she stood on tiptoe to kiss his lightly stubbled cheek as she wished him good night.

The ever present Atlanta wind whipped about her body, molding her coat to the gentle swell of her abdomen as she wearily mounted the front steps. Mike watched her until she was safely inside, then, whistling tunelessly, continued on his rounds. Neither of them had noticed the dark car parked at the curb.

Leaning heavily on the railing, Kelly made her way carefully up the three flights of stairs to her apartment—if one room could be called such. The elevator in this building was worse than useless. To use it was to risk being trapped, perhaps for hours. Tonight she had been tempted. The stairs had loomed before her, seeming to be nine flights rather than three. Common sense prevailed and she had chosen the stairs, sinking further into exhaustion with each step. Tonight she found no humor in the constantly changing graffiti that was scrawled on the walls of the stairwell.

Each step seemed to become higher. It took a conscious effort to lift her foot, shift her weight, then lift the other foot. When she was sure she could endure no more, it was over. The last step, thank God! Her apartment door beckoned to her like a haven in a sea of turmoil. Fumbling with her keys, then with the always recalcitrant lock, she managed to open the door. Inside, hidden away from any prying eyes, she sank down in the chair by the door. Spent and weary, she sat in the darkness.

There was not a part of her body that didn't ache. The new bulk of her baby had forced her to assume an unnatural posture at the piano. The results were a neck that tensed and shoulders that cramped. After years of playing, her arms should have been strong, but lately they had grown leaden and she had to push herself to make them obey. Even her fingers seemed sore from the long contact with the ivory keys. The walk home and the climb up the stairs had been the final straws. Sitting there, darkness covering her like a cloud, in the dark, she tried vainly to deny her misery.

"Quit feeling sorry for yourself," she chided. "It's simply a question of mind over matter. Ignore the pain, forget you're tired, concentrate on the baby. Everything will turn out all right. Oh, please let everything turn out all right."

Her head fell back against the wall and her eyes closed. How long she sat like that she didn't know. It was her desperate longing for sleep that roused her. She fought the urge to tumble into bed as she was and forced herself to follow her nightly routine.

Shedding her clothes as she crossed the room, she dropped them in the hamper in the tiny bathroom. While waiting for the shower water to warm, she stood before the mirror and creamed away her heavy "stage" makeup. Deciding to skip the usual shampoo, she put on her shower cap and, at last, stepped gratefully beneath the spray.

The heat of the water felt good as she rotated her head, working the kinks from her neck and shoulders, easing the strain of the day. She sighed regretfully, knowing that soon the cost of heating the water would be more than she could afford. But for now, she would enjoy it. Stretching luxuriously, she leaned against the wall, letting the water beat down on her body. Her eyes drooped, then closed. After a second of contented blankness, Scott's face swam into her consciousness. His voice rang in her ears, teasing her as he always had about her hot showers, complaining, unjustly that it took hours for the steam to dissipate.

No! Her eyes flew open and she pushed away from the wall. She wouldn't think about Scott. Not ever again! Abruptly, she turned off the water and stepped from the shower, not as refreshed as she had hoped to be. She dried her too slender body with a soft, fluffy towel left over from better days. As she slid the towel across her breasts and abdomen, she thought guiltily of her obstetrician's concern at her low weight gain. He chided her constantly for working too hard and resting too little. Yet the very fact that she was carrying small made it possible to keep her job. Even a man like Nick would perfer that she not look like an elephant at the piano.

Kelly hung up the towel and took off the shower cap, then stared thoughtfully at her image in the clouded mirror. What was it others saw in her face? What did they read in her eyes? So many people had been kind and she would be forever grateful, but she was dreadfully tired of seeing the pity in their eyes. Only Nick and Mike's family knew her story. What others thought they knew was simple conjecture.

The sound of the doorbell broke into her reverie and she hurried from the bathroom. Who could it be at this late hour? It was probably a mistake. Maybe if she ignored it, whoever it was would just go away.

She quickly slipped into her nightgown, then tied a terry cloth robe over it. The robe had fit in her slender days, but now stretched tight across her middle. At a second and more insistent ring, she went reluctantly to the door. As she opened it, she found herself staring into Scott's eyes, eyes that looked at her from the face of the elegant stranger from the bar.

"Good evening, Miss O'Brian." His look swept over her, registering surprise at her attire. "I'm Jake Caldwell. I'd like to talk to you for a moment if I might. May I come in?"

Whatever else he said, Kelly never heard. A strange lethargy stole over her as her body felt first hot, then cold. And then all was darkness as she slowly crumpled to lie unconscious at his feet.

Two

Kelly was aware of gentle hands touching her body. She felt light and giddy as strong arms lifted her and she was cradled against a powerful chest. Subconsciously, she snuggled even closer, her head resting securely against him, his heartbeat a steady rhythm beneath her ear. Valiantly she sought to rouse herself, but the words she tried to speak would not come, the eyelids she willed to open remained closed. Her body refused her commands as she drifted deeper into a curiously nebulous state that was neither conscious nor unconscious.

Jake held his burden easily. Her slender body, even with the slight bulk of her pregnancy, fit snugly in his arms. He kicked the door shut behind him, then scanned the room with a grimace. Though excruciatingly clean and orderly, it was painfully shabby. This one room was all things, living, dining, and sleeping space. There were three doors, one leading back to the hall, one that was open leading to the tiny bathroom, and the other, he supposed, was a closet.

Shrugging aside the appearance of the room, he crossed quickly to the sofa. With infinite care, he lay her down on its worn cushions. He unfolded the colorful afghan from the back of the sofa and spread it over her. As he tucked it beneath her chin, he spoke to her softly.

"Miss O'Brian?" He sat down beside her and watched her struggle to bring her mind from the depths of its retreat. He didn't know this woman, but his heart ached for her. She might be a tramp, but she seemed so vulnerable and somehow innocent. He knew he was to be her instrument of pain and, oddly, he found the idea repugnant. He touched her forehead with a cool hand.

"Kelly? Can you open your eyes for me, sweetheart?" The endearment slipped unnoticed from his lips.

Kelly felt the gentleness of a comforting hand and heard from a great distance a soft, insistent voice. The thought skittered through her mind that she should answer the poor man. He sounded so worried. She knew she should answer, but what she truly wanted was to sink back into that safe cocoon where she didn't have to think or speak. With a brain too battered by fatigue to function rationally, she wondered again who this man could be. Who was he that he called her first Miss O'Brian, then Kelly, then sweetheart . . . and looked at her through Scott's eyes?

"Scott?" She did not realize that she had spoken aloud.

"No, Miss O'Brian," a deep, quiet voice responded. "My name is Jake. Scott was my brother."

At last her body obeyed and the heavy lids flew open. As her gold-flecked amber eyes focused on him, the big callused hand that had been stroking her tumbled curls stopped, then moved away to rest lightly on his knee. She stared at him fascinated by his eyes. They were Scott's and yet not Scott's. How were they alike? How were they different? She moved restlessly, bewildered but strangely unafraid. In a city known for its crime and violence, locked in a room with a handsome stranger, she felt safe, almost content.

"Do you do this often?" His words broke the quiet of the room.

"What?"

"Faint, Miss O'Brian. Do you often faint or are you not well?" He spoke to her as though she were a confused child.

She struggled to a sitting position, ignoring the

helping hand he offered. The move brought her closer to him and her breast brushed lightly against his bent elbow. An electric awareness sparked through her and she felt a nervousness that had nothing to do with fear.

"No, Mr. Caldwell," she said wryly, trying with an alien sarcasm to hide her reaction. "I'm not ill. I'm pregnant. Perhaps you've noticed?"

"I've noticed, Miss O'Brian." He smiled in spite of himself, admiring her fighting spirit. With another look that seemed to probe the secrets of her body, he continued more gently, "I've also noticed that you're far too thin. To look at you one would never dream your pregnancy is so far advanced. Is this normal or is there a problem?"

Kelly was startled by his concern and she found herself wanting to reassure him. "I am a little thin, and it's true that I'm carrying small, but there's no danger to the baby."

"And to yourself?" The question seemed to force its way through tight lips.

Kelly didn't answer. She searched his face, puzzled. Suddenly she wanted him to go. She didn't want to answer any more questions. His concern made her feel things she wanted to forget. She wanted to have done with this so she could rest.

"Why are you here?" she burst out. "Did Scott send you?"

"In a way." He stood and walked to the window, where he stared down at the traffic below.

"What do you mean, in a way? Either he did or he didn't send you. Has he changed his mind? Does he want the baby? Is that why you're here?" She swung her feet to the floor, intending to rise. The room rocked crazily and she found herself too dizzy to move.

"I didn't come about the baby." His clipped voice was now strangely cold.

"Then what is it he wants? He certainly doesn't want me. He made that abundantly clear when he left." Her voice was shrill and she could feel her control slipping.

Jake turned to face her. There was no way to soften the blow. "Scott's dead, Miss O'Brian."

"No!" The anguished cry was ripped from her as her body began to shiver. Her eyes shimmered with unshed tears, then one crystal drop trembled on a long dark lash and fell to her cheek. It was the prelude to the storm as the last of her control gave way.

Startled by the intensity of her reaction, Jake stood unmoving for a moment. Then he stepped quickly to her. Sitting on the sofa, he pulled her close, one hand burying itself in her golden curls. Her slight body nestled instinctively against him as the torrent of tears wet his jacket. He held her patiently, waiting for the storm to abate.

Gradually her sobbing ceased. She accepted the snowy handkerchief he pressed into her hand and dried her tears, then pulled away from him.

"I don't know why that was such a shock," she said. "I think I already knew."

He didn't speak at first, but looked at her with questioning eyes. Finally he asked, "What do you mean?"

Her lips tilted in a mockery of a smile. "Earlier you said, 'Scott *was* my brother,' not is my brother."

"I see." And he did see. This was a very sharp lady. Even exhausted and half out of her mind with worry, she had caught the nuance of a single word. This situation was not what it seemed. Only a woman who was either incredibly stupid or incredibly naive would be trapped in her predicament. Kelly O'Brian was not stupid. He found himself looking at her through new eyes, more intrigued than before.

"How did he die? When?" Her self-control had been regained. She held herself rigidly in check as she huddled on the sofa's edge.

Without thinking, Jake very gently unclasped the clenched hands in her lap. He took one in his, while his free arm went about her shoulders.

"A bit over six weeks ago Scott was in an acci-

dent. His injuries were so massive that by the time
help arrived, it was too late." His eyes were bleak and
his thoughts seemed to wander. Then in a barely
audible voice he murmured, "It was too late from the
instant the car skidded over the embankment. He
died there on a hillside in the dark."

Kelly looked down at the hand that held hers. She
touched the raw, angry scars that lanced across it.
"Were you with him?"

"No, but I was first to reach him."

"Is that how you got these?"

"Yes. The car was mangled and in flames."

"Were you badly burned?"

"No."

"I'm glad." She clasped his hand tighter in hers.

"Kelly?" He waited until she lifted her eyes to his.
"Did you love Scott even after he deserted you?"

He watched as tears welled in her eyes and spilled
down her cheeks again. She made no effort to wipe
them away.

"I'm so ashamed," she whispered. "I didn't . . ."

"Shhh." Jake freed his hand from hers, and with
a gentle finger wiped away a single tear. "My dear
child, you have nothing to be ashamed of. I should
think the shame is Scott's."

"No!" The sound was a ragged cry. "I'm the
one—it was my fault!" She searched for a way to tell
him of her guilt. Would he hate her if he knew she had
never loved Scott? Could he understand how sheer
loneliness had made her so hungry for companion-
ship that she had settled for a man who needed her,
not one she loved? Would he hate her for not loving
Scott enough to hold him and keep him safe? She
flinched at the thought of the look she would see in
Jake's eyes when he knew. Dear God! She had to tell
him. But how? With a supreme effort she lifted her
pale face to his. Her golden hair brushed his chin.

"Jake." She licked dry lips and swallowed hard,
forcing herself to continue. "I have to tell you how it
was with Scott."

"No, Kelly. You owe me no explanations. It's not

for me to pass judgment." He hesitated. "There is one question I'd like to ask, if I may."

"All . . . all right."

"Was Scott aware that you were pregnant when he left?"

"Yes." She closed her eyes against the pain. Because she had not loved him enough, she had chosen the baby over Scott and now Scott was dead.

"Then why in God's name did he leave you?" Jake was furious, but not with Kelly. He wondered if he had ever known his brother at all. This was too much, even for him. "How could he have left you?"

"You don't understand." She scrubbed miserably at the wetness on her cheeks. "Scott didn't want me to have this baby. He begged me to have an abortion, but I wouldn't. I couldn't bring myself to destroy our child. No matter how he pleaded or even cried, I refused. He flew into a rage and called me selfish and hateful. He told me over and over that he never wanted to be a father, but I wouldn't listen. Finally, he said it was unfair for me to force this on him. Oh, he made it clear how he felt, he left me absolutely no illusions." Kelly's shoulders slumped in defeat; her words were painfully slow. "But like a fool, I kept hoping he would change."

"But you were wrong." The blunt words were not a question.

"Yes. Scott couldn't stand the idea of being tied down to a child, so he ran and now he's dead." Her tears stopped and she sat staring at nothing as they dried on her face. After a while she raised a hand to cover her eyes, pressing lightly as if to blot out the pain.

"If I'd listened to him maybe he would have stayed." She dropped her hand and looked at Jake with tortured eyes. "Did I kill him? Would he still be here and alive today if I'd done what he wanted?"

"Oh, Kelly, my poor sweet innocent." He gathered her shivering body close. Neither of them thought it strange that they had met only minutes before and now sat entwined in an embrace. "Sweetheart, Scott

was charming and appealing. He could be devastatingly attentive, but there was a dark side to his
character. He was cruelly self-centered and danger-
ously irresponsible. He—" Kelly jerked from his arms,
leaping to her feet even as her hand cracked across
his cheek.

"How dare you? How dare you speak so of your
brother? This was my fault, not his." She strode to
the window, and now it was she who stared down at
the dimly lit streets.

Jake's eyes narrowed as he looked at her in
astonishment and confusion. Where there should
have been bitterness, he had seen an emotion he
could not fathom. He couldn't know that when she
struck him, she was lashing out at her own guilt. She
heard on his lips the words she had denied herself.
The words she had refused to utter. The words that
would have eased her pain. She steadfastly refused to
paint Scott black in order to ease her own conscience.

Because he could not know the turmoil that
raged within her, he drew the only conclusion he
could. Kelly must love Scott so much that even after
all he had done to her, she still couldn't bear to hear
anyone speak disparagingly of him.

"He can't be blamed because I got pregnant," she
murmured. "Guaranteed more than ninety percent
effective, but"—she laughed mirthlessly and looked
down at her protruding abdomen—"not for me. If
only I had listened to him and had the abortion, he
might still be alive. No matter what has happened, he
was kind to me, Jake, and I did this to him."

"No!" He had quietly crossed the room to her,
shaking his head in wonder. He couldn't believe what
he was hearing. How could she think this way? What
was she, actress, martyr, or just blindly, lovingly
loyal? Again a quiet rage at Scott filled his heart. He
placed his hands on her shoulders and turned her to
face him. He could read nothing in her carefully blank
face.

"How can you defend him? How can you call him
kind when he left you alone and pregnant? Was it

kindness to insist you have an abortion? Or when he left you almost penniless?" His eyes swept the room again, registering disgust. "Haven't you realized yet that Scott was a wealthy man? He could easily have provided for you."

Kelly searched his face and saw pain there. For the first time, she realized how much it cost Jake to say these things about his brother. Still she stubbornly insisted, "Yes, he was kind to me. At least while he was here, he was kind."

"Kelly." Jake hesitated, then spoke gently. "No man who is kind has an affair with a woman, then leaves her alone when she's pregnant with his child."

"Affair!" She stared at him, aghast. "Is that what you're thinking? You think that poor brother Scott got himself involved with a tramp and now she's pregnant?"

She whirled away from him and crossed the room. An old family Bible sat on a table, and from it she drew out a paper. "Do you see this? It's a marriage certificate. Scott and I were married last December."

Kelly stepped forward, the paper held tightly in her hand. "It's written here in black and white that Jason Scott Caldwell and Kelly Marie O'Brian are married. Don't you *dare* accuse me of having an affair with your brother!"

"May I see that?" Jake said quietly.

"Certainly. Do you doubt my word?" She thrust the paper at him and watched as he unfolded it.

Impassively, he read the certificate, betraying none of the shock he felt as he read the names on it.

"Are you satisfied?" Kelly asked. "Did you really think I would lie about something so important? Perhaps it wasn't a good marriage, but like it or not, I was married to your brother."

"No, Kelly, you weren't." He calmly refolded the certificate.

"You don't know me, Jake, so I can understand that you might not believe me. I—I can see how you might think I made it all up because of the baby. But how can you deny the truth of what's written there?"

He stood looking at her for a long while, his expression unreadable.

"Oh, never mind!" she snapped, her patience at an end. "It really doesn't matter what you believe. It doesn't matter in the least." The tenuous control she had sought to maintain slipped and her voice broke badly on the last word.

"Kelly, I never said I didn't believe you, not once."

"You did! You said—"

"No." He spoke gently. "I said you weren't married to my brother. This paper, as you have said, states in black and white that you are married to me."

Kelly raised stunned eyes to meet his. His slate blue eyes, looking steadily into hers, held no mockery, only compassion. Again her resolve faltered and she looked away from a gaze that saw too much.

"This is crazy!" she whispered. "I've just met you. I'm—I'm married to Scott."

"No, Kelly."

"If this is a joke, it's not very funny," she muttered.

"It's no joke, I assure you." There was a very real tenderness in his low voice. "It's true, Kelly. Scott and I were fraternal twins. Our names were the same in reverse. He was Scott Jason, I'm Jason Scott. The name on the marriage certificate is mine."

He reached out suddenly to steady her. She had grown so pale that he feared she might faint again. He could feel her violent trembling. Hoping to reassure her, he said softly, "Perhaps it's a mistake. Some fool clerk must have inadvertently reversed the names."

He didn't mention that the signature on the certificate was also his, a perfect forgery. It was a skill that Scott had long ago learned, though used until now only for boyish pranks.

Her last illusion destroyed, Kelly let him hold her. At this point she had no will of her own. From far away she heard his voice speaking softly. Only his suggestion of an error pierced her thoughts.

"There was no mistake," she said sadly, looking up at Jake. "He said his name was Jason Scott, and even explained that he was called Scott because his father's name was the same. It kept down the confusion."

"Oh, hell!" Jake pressed her gently to his chest. He couldn't bear the emptiness in her eyes.

"It's really true, isn't it?" she murmured in a ragged voice. "Why did he do this to me?"

Jake hesitated, dreading the additional pain he knew he must cause her, then spoke as gently as he could. "Perhaps it was because he already had a wife."

Kelly's blood turned cold. A sharp pain shot through her, leaving a ragged throbbing in its wake. It was an effort to breathe. She almost wished her last breath had been drawn. She swayed on her feet and would have fallen if not for Jake's strong arms.

"I'm sorry, Kelly," he murmured against her hair. "I didn't mean to be so blunt."

An unnatural laugh bubbled in her throat as horror and hysteria gripped her. Her head turned rhythmically from side to side as peal after peal of mirthless laughter spilled from her.

"Stop it, Kelly. Stop!" He shook her by the shoulders, at first gently, then harder. Her neck snapped back painfully and the laughter stopped. Now she stared at him with unfocused eyes, lost in a hysterical trance more frightening than the laughter.

"Oh, sweet Kelly." He groaned as he pulled her rigid body into his arms. His mouth brushed hers softly, then insistently. With tender care he teased and coaxed her cold, stiff lips until they softened and parted. She whimpered and her arms crept around his body, urgently clasping his waist in response. But her response was passionless, one of a wounded soul to a healing force. After a time, slowly, reluctantly, he released her. Brushing back her shining curls, he told himself sternly that the kiss had been a means to break the hysteria, nothing more. He fiercely denied the feelings surging through him. Yet he knew he desperately wanted to kiss her again, to hold her and ease her pain.

Kelly O'Brian—no, Kelly Caldwell—was not a tramp as he had first suspected. She had had no vicious claws in his brother, but had instead been his victim. With a single finger beneath her chin, he lifted her head. He searched her face but found no hint of lingering hysteria. But now, for the first time, there was bitterness written on her sweet features.

"Come, sit down." He led her to the two faded chairs in the corner of the room. "Do you have any brandy?"

"Yes. It was Sc—his. I don't drink it," she mumbled.

"Tonight you do. Where is it?"

"In the kitchen, in the cabinet over the refrigerator."

Jake stepped to the cabinet. He found the bottle and two glasses. He poured a small amount of brandy into one glass and a more generous amount into the other for himself.

"Drink it," he commanded as he pressed the glass into her hand.

She sipped tentatively, making a face at the unpleasant taste.

"Drink all of it. You need it." He sat down in the other chair, watching as she obeyed with a grimace.

"Jake"—she stared down at her empty glass—"how did you find me? Surely Scott didn't just casually say, 'Oh, by the way I have a second wife in Atlanta.'"

"Don't, Kelly. Don't do this to yourself. Just accept it that I did find you."

"No. I want to know. Did he tell you about me?" she continued stubbornly.

"No, only your name."

"When?"

"Kelly, please don't."

"When?"

A long pause followed. Jake found it harder and

harder not to take her back into his arms. He wanted to kiss her, not hurt her more.

"Answer me, Jake."

With a sigh he answered, his eyes closed against the pain he knew he would see. "It was as he was dying."

"So." Her laugh was brittle. "If it hadn't been for a deathbed confession, you would never have known about me."

"I'm sorry."

"Don't be." With nervous fingers she smoothed away an invisible wrinkle in her robe, then folded her hands, willing them to be still. Her voice was steady when she spoke again. "I'd still like to know how you found me."

"There was a photograph among Scott's papers. The investigator recognized a landmark and took it from there."

"Then I was only a name to him, nothing more." Fresh pain trembled through her. How much more was there? Could she bear it?

Jake leaned forward to take one of her cold hands in his. "I really think he was sorry for what he had done to you. He asked me to find you and help you. That's why I'm here, Kelly, to help you."

She didn't pull her hand away. She looked unblinkingly at the man before her. How could she know that this man would be strong when Scott had been weak, true when Scott had been false? How could she, when she had been so wrong about one man, be so confident about another? She didn't understand how she knew, but nevertheless she knew.

"You've done this before, haven't you?" Her look was shrewd, her voice hard. "You've had to solve problems created by Scott before."

Jake hesitated, knowing his answer would wound again. "Yes, I've done it before," he answered quietly.

"Then there have been a lot of women."

"Yes."

"Were there other children?" Her voice broke again. This time the pain threatened to consume her.

"No, Kelly, there were no other children."

"I suppose that, at least, is a relief. I mean, how does one go about sweeping dozens of bastard children under the carpet?" She was mocking both herself and him with her cruelty now.

"Most of Scott's women knew the score."

"Most, but not all. Am I right?" she asked with a false sweetness that hurt him. "Answer me, Jake."

Reluctantly he agreed. "Most, but not all."

"How many? How many others were the fool I've been?"

"Only one other." He gripped her hand hard. "Leave it alone, Kelly. Don't keep doing this to yourself."

"Who was she?" Her voice was guttural, her body growing more and more rigid. "Who was she?"

"His wife, Lydia."

"He hurt her just as he has me?"

"Yes, perhaps even more."

Kelly sat still for a long while. Jake didn't intrude on her thoughts. He leaned back in his chair and watched the various emotions cross her face. From all that had transpired in this room in the last hour, he understood the ravaged state of her mind. Which way would her thoughts take her? Only she could decide, and Jake felt he owed her the time to come to her own conclusions.

"Yes," she said, nodding, as if seeing the situation from another angle. "I can see that what he's done to her was even more cruel than anything he might have done to me." Again she fell silent, and again Jake waited.

Only the ticking of the clock by her chair broke the silence. Then with a newfound resolve she made her decision. When she spoke at last, her voice was once more low and controlled. Out of pain and deep humiliation had come her natural serenity.

"I can't undo the harm Scott has done his wife,

but I can spare her more pain. I promise you that she will never know about this child."

"Do you mean that?" Somehow he wasn't surprised. His opinion of her had undergone many changes in the last hour. Now he knew her to be a compassionate person, sensitive to the pain or happiness of others.

"Of course I mean it. I'd get no pleasure in telling her that I'm having—" Her voice faltered and sank to a pain-filled whisper. "Having her husband's baby."

Her hands protectively covered her stomach. She moaned. "My poor baby, how can I ever explain why you have no father?" Her arms tightened convulsively about herself as she rocked back and forth, a single tear trickling down her face.

"You won't have to." Jake spoke quietly, but with conviction. "The baby will be mine."

Kelly's head jerked up with a snap, her incredulous eyes asking the question her befuddled mind could not formulate.

"The certificate says that you *are* my wife. From this moment, as far as the world is concerned, I married you last December and it's my child you carry." He smiled as she stared at him blankly. "Don't be frightened, I won't make any demands on you. This will be for the sake of the child, and to spare my family any further hurt."

"But, Jake, you can't—" she began, only to be interrupted by his stern voice.

"Think about it, Kelly. Think before you decide. This baby deserves its inheritance as well as its father's name. Our trusts, Scott's and mine, stipulate that if either of us dies without children, the bulk of his estate goes to the firstborn of the other. This is the only solution. The baby will receive its inheritance and I can care for you. No one need ever know the truth."

"And his wife?"

"She'll be well taken care of and will certainly never want for anything. At this point, my greatest concern is you."

"But this is crazy. You don't even know me! I don't know you. No. It won't work, it couldn't," she said adamantly.

"Kelly, Kelly." He leaned forward to take both her hands back into his. "It will work. We'll make it work. We can treat it as a business arrangement, an investment in the baby's future. It will also give my mother a chance to enjoy the grandchild she's always wanted. Think about it, Kelly. Think long and hard. Be very sure before you make your decision."

He smiled crookedly at her. "You're dead on your feet." He rose, then paused to stroke her cheek with one finger. "Rest now, if you can, and I'll be back about ten o'clock tomorrow morning."

In a move that had become almost a habit, he brushed her curls back from her forehead and murmured, "Good night, Kelly."

The door closed softly behind him but Kelly remained seated, her mind too muddled by all that had happened, by all that had been said. Finally, knowing she could stay awake no longer, she opened her sofa bed and, climbing wearily between the sheets, fell almost instantly into the deep but restless sleep of exhaustion.

Three

The soft insistent rapping at the door woke her. She pulled herself from a dreamworld filled with men, all of whom had the same eyes. They danced and whirled through her sleep as the names Jason Scott and Scott Jason were chanted endlessly, over and over.

"Kelly?" a muffled voice called as the rapping became more demanding. "Kelly? Are you all right in there?" The doorknob rattled fiercely. "Kelly! Answer me!"

The chill of the night air lingered in the room, making her reluctant to leave her warm bed. Yet she knew she must, for Jake showed no signs of leaving. With hurried movements, she threw back the covers and grabbed her robe.

"I'm coming," she grumbled as she tied the belt around her. She flew across the cold floor and unlocked the door.

It swung open to reveal a casually dressed and heavily laden Jake. His eyes, gleaming down at her, were like the morning sky. His jaw was freshly shaven and his carefully slicked-down hair was already beginning to struggle back into its abounding natural curl. He wore tight dark jeans and a brilliantly red sweater, with white collar and cuffs showing at his neck and wrists. From the bag in his arms emanated the most delicious aroma of freshly ground coffee and newly baked cinnamon rolls.

"Good morning," Kelly said softly, now suddenly shy. "Come in." She scurried back to the bed and retrieved her slippers that peeked out from under it.

"Good lord, woman!" Jake exclaimed as he stepped further into the room. "It's like a refrigerator in here. It's warmer outside."

He pushed the door shut with his foot, then strode across the room to the kitchen area. In exasperation he set the bag down on the counter then turned.

Kelly watched him curiously as his keen gaze scanned the room, missing nothing. He paused for a moment and nodded curtly, then swiftly walked to the far wall where the thermostat was.

"Why is your heat turned off?" he demanded. "Even Atlanta nights can be chilly this time of year."

She clutched the lapels of her robe tightly to her, trying not to shiver. "What business is it of yours what stupid temperature I set my thermostat on?"

"Stop acting like a child, Kelly," he said with little patience. "It's turned all the way down. Why?"

A shiver quaked through her despite all her efforts to suppress it. Her pride wouldn't let her reach for the afghan, though she longed for its added warmth. To still her trembling legs, she sat on the edge of the bed, all the while keeping her chin tilted at a defiant angle, mutely refusing to answer his imperious question. Never would she admit that turning off her heat at night was an economic necessity. Unconsciously, her chin lifted another notch.

"Damn stubborn woman!" Jake grumbled, frightened of what a chill could do to her. She appeared so frail and the pregnancy had taken its toll. He shuddered to think what a common cold might do to her physical reserves. He suddenly wheeled around and strode into the bathroom.

Now violently shivering, Kelly could hear several muffled sounds, then the shower began to run forcefully. Wearing a grim expression, Jake stepped back into the room.

"Go take a warm shower. I'll turn up the heat. Hopefully by the time you're through, this room will be a little less arctic. When you've thawed and dressed, we'll have breakfast and talk."

She really wanted to refuse on principle, but the lure of the hot, steaming shower was more than she could resist. Almost without thinking, she pulled some clothes from her closet. At the bathroom door she hesitated, her lower lip caught between her teeth, a frown on her face.

"Don't worry, Kelly," Jake said, grinning. "Molesting fat little women is not exactly my cup of tea."

"I'm not fat!" she retorted. "Merely pregnant." She slammed the bathroom door behind her, missing his muttered agreement and the flicker of concern that crossed his face.

Twenty minutes and an entire tank of hot water later, Kelly emerged, flushed a delicate pink from a combination of scrubbing, hot water, and shyness. She had dressed in a pair of elastic-waisted gray slacks and a loose fitting blouse, whose varying shades of mauve complemented her eyes, turning them a deep shade of golden brown. She smoothed the blouse down over her abdomen. One good thing about carrying small was that she didn't have to invest in any maternity clothes. That in itself had saved a great deal of her rapidly diminishing funds.

"Good. You're through," Jake said, glancing at her over his shoulder. He was setting the table in the kitchen area. "Sit down here. Breakfast won't be a minute."

"But I don't eat—" She clamped her jaw shut, biting off the words. She normally didn't eat breakfast, but this time she decided not to make an issue of it.

She sat down and Jake set a plate filled with scrambled eggs and crisp bacon before her. There was also juice, coffee, and the marvelously fragrant cinnamon rolls. He got his plate and sat down across from her to eat with obvious relish.

"Jake."

"Shhh. Eat your breakfast while it's hot. We'll talk later."

"But—"

"Kelly, eat your breakfast." He spoke patiently but firmly, his tone permitting no argument.

She picked up her fork and reluctantly began to eat. She wouldn't be able to manage this, she thought. She had never liked breakfast. She ate with stubborn determination, then was more than a little astonished to find that she had eaten all of her bacon and eggs and two of the rolls for good measure. Sighing, she leaned back in her chair, content to watch as Jake finished off the last of the rolls.

"For a little girl who doesn't eat breakfast, you did quite well," he said. "You wouldn't be hiding a truck driver beneath that delicate exterior, would you?" He stood and reached for her plate. "I'll do the dishes. It won't take long. Go sit and rest for a while. When I'm through, we'll have our talk."

Kelly didn't protest. The lethargy and constant sleepiness that had plagued her throughout her pregnancy was threatening to overwhelm her completely. She settled into one of the armchairs with a paperback novel, intending to read for a few minutes. But she spent more time watching Jake than she did reading. Then quite without realizing what was happening, she drifted into a contented sleep.

She slept so deeply that she wasn't aware when the sounds from the kitchen area stopped. Nor did she hear Jake cross the room to stand over her, watching, pleased that she rested. She did not know that his fingers tingled with the need to touch her satiny smooth cheek. Nor did she know that he ached to press his lips to her neck, so very sweetly exposed as her head drooped forward in an easy slumber. None of this intruded on her peaceful dream. It was the book being carefully removed from her fingers that woke her.

"What . . . ?" She roused herself with an effort.

"Sorry, darling. I didn't mean to wake you."

"Scott?"

"No."

Reality came flooding back. Scott was gone. Forever. He had left her pregnant and alone. No! She was no longer alone. Jake had come.

"I'm sorry, Jake. I didn't mean to fall asleep. But lately, I either fall asleep or cry at the drop of a hat." Her apologetic voice was soft with traces of lingering confusion.

Jake looked down at her with an unfathomable expression, then his lips softened into a smile. "Don't feel you need to apologize to me. You're tired and alone, but I'm here now to change that. And don't you forget it, sleepyhead." With a chuckle, he tapped her lightly on her upturned nose.

He sprawled gracefully in the chair across from her. In the back of her mind she realized that not only had he cleaned the kitchen, but had closed the sofa bed as well. Even the afghan and bedclothes had been neatly folded.

"Have you given any more thought to my suggestion?" he asked quietly, his penetrating eyes focused intently on her face.

"Not—not really. I thought once the shock had worn off you'd be thinking more clearly and would change your mind." Her restless fingers folded and pleated the loose ends of her blouse. Her eyes could not meet his.

"I don't deny that it was a shock. But I haven't changed my mind." His voice was expressionless and she could read nothing, absolutely nothing, in his words.

"Look." She let go of the folded fabric, then stroked the wrinkles from it. "This really isn't your problem. Whatever mistakes Scott and I made, they're no concern of yours. And though I really do appreciate—"

"Kelly." He captured a nervous hand. "Look at me. Don't drop your head. This whole affair is none of your doing. Don't refuse my help, please." He waited, but still she kept her eyes on her hand, clasped safely in his.

"Kelly, look at me." A command, but gently given. He waited patiently until she raised her eyes to his.

"For all our differences, Scott and I were brothers. We quarreled and fought as all children do, and in later years we drifted apart as our lives took different paths. But one thing never changed—we loved each other. There were times when I didn't like Scott, and times when he felt the same about me. But the bond was always there. Perhaps only another twin could understand the depth of the feeling we shared. Sometimes I wondered if even we understood." Jake paused and shifted slightly in his chair.

"We were something of a paradox. When we reached our teens my body began to spurt up and out, while Scott remained small and slight. It was I who beat my head in on the football field and on the collegiate wrestling mat. These were all things Scott wanted to do, but he was too small. He resented what he considered were great accomplishments and became very bitter. And all the while I would have traded all I had to be able to do what he could with brush and paints. Did you ever see any of his watercolors?"

Kelly didn't speak, only shook her head, not wanting to interrupt his fascinating narrative. She realized that she was being given a rare insight into both men.

"No? I don't suppose that should surprise me. He refused to recognize his own abilities, nor would he ever admit that he had talents that far surpassed mine. Kelly, he was absolutely amazing. With a little paint he could make a few squiggles on canvas and a sunset would come to life, or water would flow. I swear sometimes you could almost smell the flowers. But time after time I've seen him destroy drawings that were breathtaking. I think—" He paused at his next words, as though the admission hurt. "I think at those times I came closest to hating him. How could anybody with such a talent not use it? He could have given the world so much beauty, could have made it a better place simply by bringing joy with his paintings." Jake stood and paced the room restlessly. Kelly watched him quietly and waited.

"All his life Scott thought only of himself. Never once until now can I remember him showing concern for anyone other than himself. If you'd known him better, you would understand how out of character it was for him to ask me to help you." Jake returned to her chair, grasping her hands again. In a low urgent voice, he tried to make her understand.

"Kelly, Scott was so badly hurt. The pain must have been unbearable, yet his thoughts were of you. At the worst time of his entire life, he was thinking of someone else. He was acting like the man he could have been. His last minutes, when he asked me to help you, were the best in his life. Can't you see that by doing as he asked, I can make his life less a waste, and his death less a tragedy? For the first time he wanted to make right a wrong he had inflicted. Before, he had never cared. If for no other reason than to make his life have meaning, let me help you."

Kelly dropped her head. During Jake's long and moving speech her eyes had never left his face. She had seen suffering and grief, and even futility written there. Now at his last plea, she could bear no more. Her tender heart went out to both Jake and Scott. Tears began to trickle down her face. How very sad that as boys each had been what the other wanted to be. Jake had accepted his lot and made the most of what he had. Scott had grown self-centered and bitter.

"Kelly." Jake's big hand caressed her face. "Don't cry for us, love. You've already shed too many tears because of the Caldwells." He stroked the tears away with his thumb, waiting patiently. He would say no more until she was once again in control.

After a minute, she turned her head into the palm of his hand and smiled weakly at him. It was as though she caressed him with her eyes.

Jake steeled himself against the desire to take her in his arms and forced himself to continue. "Will you let me help? Not because we owe you something, but for Scott's sake. To make his life have some value after all."

"What about your life?" She shook her head slightly and his hand fell away. "Why should you tie yourself to me and to this baby? Surely you'll want a family of your own one day."

"At the moment, there's nothing happening in my life. There's no special person. I'm footloose and fancy-free." He was trying to tease, but his smile was ignored.

"But what about the future? We can't pretend it will all take care of itself," she insisted.

"This doesn't have to be forever. Just a few months should accomplish our purpose and your baby will be Scott's legal heir. Once you're completely recovered from the baby's birth, you'll be free to go. I won't try to keep you. All I ask is that my mother have access to her grandchild."

"Then what you're saying is that from now until the baby is born, we'll pretend to be married. Then after a few months we'll separate, supposedly for the second time."

"Yes."

"Can we do it?"

"I don't see why not. We need only to plan our strategy very carefully and make it believable."

"Jake, I don't want your money, but I would like more than anything in the world for my baby to have a father . . . even if it's only pretend."

Jake saw a shadow cross her face. "Why is having a father for your baby more important than having financial security? There's no stigma attached to being the child of a single parent today. Nowadays it's an accepted fact of life."

"Not to me it isn't!" she snapped. "I don't care what the fashion is, it hurts to be illegitimate. I know."

"Then you were illegitimate?"

"Yes."

"Did you ever know your father?"

"How could I?" Her voice was filled with bitterness. "Even my mother wasn't sure which of her lovers it was."

"Dear God!" Jake exclaimed. "Kelly, you, above all people, must understand why we should go ahead with my plan." He waited for her to respond, but she sat mutely.

"Will you, Kelly?" he asked quietly. "Will you do this for both of us?"

A shuddering breath caught in her throat. She hesitated, not knowing what to do for she was desperately confused.

"Kelly?"

"Yes . . . yes, I'll do it." The words tumbled from her lips in a frantic rush.

"Good. You won't regret it. I promise." He kissed her lightly on the lips then, oblivious to her shocked expression and the blush that stained her face, he stood up.

"You take it easy for the rest of the day. I'll get some things arranged, then pick you up and drive you to work at . . . ?"

"Seven."

"Right, seven. I'll see you then. After you get off work we'll make some definite plans." At her nod, he smiled and walked to the door. There he paused.

"Kelly." He waited until she looked fully at him. "Thank you."

The door closed behind him, leaving Kelly stunned. What a complex man he was. He had stepped into her life, shouldered all her problems, and then he thanked her! She shook her head in wonder.

That night she played with a flair and style that was rare even for her, as her slender fingers flew over the keyboard. Her smile sparkled brighter than ever and often her eyes strayed to the man sitting at the table nearest the piano. Could this really be happening? Could this man have stepped into her life and so easily swept away all her worries? Jake. Was he real? She glanced at his table. Yes, he was real, very much so. She smiled. His answering smile made her heart skip a beat.

As he made one of his nightly walks among the tables to greet his customers and friends, Nick passed Jake's table. Kelly saw Jake speak and Nick paused. Something Jake said seemed to startle Nick, then a slow, pleased smile spread across his lips. He pulled a chair out and sat, head inclined as Jake continued speaking.

Kelly played steadily for the next fifteen minutes, all the while wondering what the two men found so engrossing. Then Nick rose, offered Jake his hand, and patted him on the shoulder as he walked away.

Kelly played some more requests and talked to several of her favorite customers. Try as she might she couldn't keep her eyes from wandering more and more often to Jake's table.

"Kelly?"

"Oh, hi, Nick. I didn't see you standing there." Her dimple flashed even deeper than usual.

"Could I see you in my office for a minute?"

"Now?"

Nick checked his watch. "Let's say at ten o'clock. That's ten minutes from now."

"Okay." Kelly was very curious. She had another hour to play before quitting. Nick had never interrupted her before.

For the next few minutes she played mechanically, her mind not on her music. Consequently, she made mistakes. When the time was up and she finished her last song, she looked up again at Jake's table.

A cold fear clutched at her heart and a pain she didn't understand lanced through her when she saw his empty chair. All her newfound hopes were suddenly dashed to the ground. Had her indecision driven him away? He had offered so much and asked so little, and like a fool she had hesitated. Had her reluctant agreement to his proposition not been enough? Dear heaven, what would she do now? The usual weariness that had been absent tonight came over her again, covering her like a cloak.

Without closing the piano, Kelly left the bench

and made her way through the tables to the door of Nick's office. She tapped lightly, then waited.

"Come."

"Nick, is something wro—" She halted abruptly. Nick sat at his desk, but her attention was captured by the man who lounged indolently in a chair by the window. A great joy lifted her spirits and her heart became a trip-hammer.

"Come on in, Kelly," Nick said. "Shut the door." His eyes darted from Kelly to Jake.

She carefully closed the door, then walked on wobbly legs to a chair across from Nick.

"I know the whole story, Kelly." Nick spoke without preamble, but gently. "Jake explained the situation. His solution sounds like a good one, but if it's not what you want, I'll help you any way I can."

"Thank you, Nick, but you've already been too kind. I've agreed to Jake's plan. It seems to be the best solution, at least for the baby and me." Kelly forced herself not to look at Jake as she spoke. She wondered why he hadn't spoken. Why did he sit in the shadows watching her so closely?

"Kelly, be sure this is what you want. Don't make a hasty decision you might regret," Nick persisted.

She raised her eyes and looked at Jake for the first time. Her voice held more conviction than she felt. "I'm sure."

"Good." Nick smacked his hands down on his desk. "I'll miss you, kid. Let me hear from you, and if you ever need anything just yell, and I'll be there." He stood up and smiled fondly at her. "You better call it a night. Jake says you'll be leaving tomorrow."

"But I can't leave so soon," she said in a sudden panic. "You have to have time to find a replacement for me first."

"I can always get another piano player. Granted, there'll never be another Kelly O'Brian, but piano players are a dime a dozen and you know it."

"But it's no—"

"Don't argue, Kelly." Jake's voice cut across the room. "Get your coat, we're leaving."

"I can't leave now," she answered stubbornly. "There are some people I want to say good-bye to. I can't just walk out without a word."

"How long will it take?" Jake asked impatiently. "Will half an hour be long enough?"

"No. Mike won't be here until eleven. I can't leave before then." She tilted her chin at a dangerous angle, daring him to deny her this.

"Then say your good-byes. I'll be waiting in the car." After a quick handshake with Nick, Jake left without another word.

It was more than a little after eleven when Kelly joined Jake in the car. Mike had kept her longer than she'd expected, questioning her about this decision. He was afraid she was making a mistake. Because of Scott, Mike had little love for the Caldwells. Though he didn't try to change her mind, he made it clear that he had strong reservations. Gently, as was his way, he reminded her that he and Kathleen would always be there if she ever needed them. Kelly went into his arms then, thinking this must be how it felt to have a father. The soft kiss she brushed on his cheek was damp with tears. She left him there to join Jake, who was leaning against his car.

As she approached, she felt his keen eyes sweeping over her. Because of his strange and withdrawn attitude, she had resisted the impulse to introduce him to Mike. Mike's reservations would have grown stronger rather than been relieved had he met this morose stranger. Solemnly, without speaking, Jake opened the car door for her.

The ride to her apartment was a short one, but the silence made it seem interminable. Jake was so aloof. When he had driven her to work earlier, he had been in a light mood, laughing and teasing her. Now he had changed. Why?

"He's old enough to be your father." Jake's cold voice knifed through the thickening silence.

"Nick?"

"No, Mike," he growled, his eyes never leaving the road.

"Yes, that's true, but then his wife's old enough to be my mother too." Was she wrong or did Jake's dark expression soften slightly? Too tired to think about it anymore, Kelly closed her eyes and slid down to rest her head on the back of the seat.

"Sleepy?"

"A bit."

"What are you thinking, Kelly?"

She shifted uncomfortably, not wanting to share her thoughts with him. Then, making her voice as light as she could, she said, "Oh, everything and nothing."

"That's no answer," he muttered, but he said no more. When they stopped in front of her apartment building, he didn't immediately get out of the car. Kelly didn't move either, but waited to take her cue from him.

"Tell me what's wrong, Kelly." He gripped the steering wheel tightly and didn't look at her.

"I don't know." She dropped her head, feeling miserable.

Jake turned and stared at her for a long while, his eyes seeming to burn into her. She tried unsuccessfully not to show her agitation and Jake's frown did nothing to reassure her.

"We need to talk, don't we?" he asked.

"Yes." Her voice quavered slightly. "I suppose we do."

Jake got out of the car abruptly, and before she knew it, she was up the front steps and in the lobby. He cocked an eye at the elevator and she smiled in spite of herself.

"I wouldn't dare," she said, "but you go ahead. I'll send the rescue team if you get stuck."

He only smiled and took her arm to lead her to the stairs. For the first two flights they climbed side by side, but at the beginning of the third her pace slowed perceptibly. Without warning, Jake scooped her up into his arms.

"Jake, put me down!"

"No."

"You can't do this."

"I *am* doing it."

"This is ridiculous. I can walk, you know."

"Shut up, Kelly, and enjoy the graffiti." He smiled down at her as he carried her with ease.

Even a woman as stubborn as Kelly had to admit it was good to be in the arms of a man so strong. With a sigh, she relaxed and leaned her head against his shoulder. His chuckle rumbled in her ear.

"You're quite a woman, Kelly Caldwell," he murmured.

A shiver of pleasure coursed through her. It was not only for the words he spoke, or that he called her Kelly Caldwell for the first time. It was for the admiration she heard in his voice.

Jake took the steps two at a time, her weight negligible in his arms. For a moment, Kelly wished it had been the strong twin rather than the weak who had come into her life first. She squelched the thought rapidly, realizing in that direction lay bitterness. She must not allow herself to dwell on the past. She must look to the future and its promise.

"Is your key in your purse?"

Lost in her thoughts, Kelly had been unaware that they had reached her door.

"If you'll put me down, I'll get it."

"No need, I can do it. Just hand me the key." He took the key she managed to extract from her purse and, with an ease that amazed her, opened the door in only one try.

"I can never do that."

"Can never do what?" he asked, mildly curious at her wistful expression.

"You opened that door with a simple twist of your wrist. It takes me at least three tries and a lot of pulling and tugging too."

"After tonight"—he pushed the door open with his shoulder and stepped into the dark room—"you won't need to worry about that particular lock anymore."

With the surefootedness of a cat, he crossed to

the sofa, set her down easily, then reached for the lamp. Its soft light flooded the room.

"Here, let me take your coat. Do you feel like talking now, or would you rather have a shower and change first?"

He caught the slight smile that crossed her lips. "What are you smiling about? Did I say something funny?"

"I was just thinking," she said, "that each time I've seen you, if I haven't just come from the shower, you're putting me into it."

"I only put you in the shower once," he declared, "and that was to thaw you out, if you'll remember." His eyes sparkled.

Jake tossed her coat over a chair, then sat down beside her. His expression sobered. "These last few minutes have been nice, but we both got off the track earlier this evening, didn't we?"

"Yes, I suppose we did. But I really don't understand what happened," she murmured.

"I think I do."

Kelly looked at him questioningly. She had no idea what he meant.

"We weren't communicating, Kelly. If this is to work, we always have to keep our lines of communication clear."

"How do we do that?"

"By being totally open with each other. By asking questions when we don't understand . . . and by giving honest answers."

"Can we be totally honest when this whole relationship is built on a lie?" she asked doubtfully.

"In the strictest sense of the word, it's not a lie. Have you forgotten? The marriage certificate bears my name."

"It's something I'm not likely to forget ever. . . ."

"Shhh. Don't think about that now. Let's put the past where it belongs and deal with the present." He touched her neck where her curls tumbled in a golden riot. "Let's start with tonight. Tell me what upset you."

She hesitated, not knowing where to begin. She knew he was right, but total honesty wasn't always easy. There were some truths with which one couldn't cope.

"Kelly, don't be frightened. There's nothing you can't ask or tell me."

She looked away and spoke in a whisper. "There's nothing specific I can point out. It was more a feeling, something I sensed rather than something you did."

"What was it you sensed?"

"Withdrawal," she answered promptly. "Without warning you seemed distant and cool, and I could think of only one reason for it."

"And what reason was that?"

"I thought—" she looked at him now "—that you had changed your mind about me."

"I see." He began massaging her tired neck. "We really have been at cross-purposes, haven't we? That's exactly how I've been feeling tonight. I was afraid you would change *your* mind. It occurred to me that with Nick and Mike, you might not need me."

"I haven't changed my mind," she said softly.

"Neither have I." He stopped the absentminded massaging and tousled her hair. "Now that we have that settled you go take your shower. I'll make some coffee and sandwiches." She laughed and he smiled. "I like to hear you laugh, Kelly. I'll have to see that you do it more often. Now, scoot. We've a lot of planning to do."

Four

"All set? You haven't forgotten anything?"

"I haven't forgotten a thing. I'm ready when you are."

Jake smiled, pleased at how rested Kelly looked as she leaned back into the soft, luxurious seat of the Seville. She had been surprised the night before when he'd called an abrupt halt in the midst of their planning, insisting that she get to bed early in preparation for the busy day ahead.

Determinedly and firmly ignoring her protests, he had opened her sofa bed, efficiently snapping sheets into place and plumping pillows. Her protests had died on her lips when he'd fixed her with a commanding look, promising he would dress her for bed himself if she didn't do as he asked.

"Asked?" she'd retorted.

"Don't push it, woman. Dressing fat, little ladies for bed could easily become one of my favorite pastimes," he teased.

Color had flamed in her face as she snatched the ancient flannel gown from him and scurried to the safety of the bathroom. His gentle laughter had followed her, a pleasant sound that swept away her anger. But the memory of the strangely tender look that had accompanied his quiet threat lingered, tantalizing her.

He had been right. In this busy day, the extra rest had stood her in good stead, making it fun, rather than tiring. They had started with an early morning shopping trip and ended at her apartment where Jake had adamantly told her to sit, watch, and supervise as he packed her things. Under her direction, he separated everything into two groups. One they would take with them, the other would be picked up later by a delivery service. It surprised Kelly to see how very little she had. Aside from her clothing, a few mementos, her books and her music, she really had nothing. She would be taking a bit of Atlanta with her, memories both good and bad, and the love of a few treasured friends.

Today was the first day of the new life she hoped to create for her unborn child. It was an end and a beginning. It was time to go. She smiled at Jake as he put the car in gear and pulled away from the curb. The traffic was light, the rush hour long over.

"Hey, don't be sad," Jake said. Not fooled by her smile, he touched her cheek tenderly. "We'll be back before you know it. Remember, I promised Kathleen I would bring you for a visit as soon as you and the baby are able to travel."

A small glimmer shone in her eyes as she remembered the early afternoon visit to the Cannons. When Jake had learned how kind they had been to her, he'd insisted that he meet them and thank them. For Kathleen and Jake, it had been instant love. Mike had been slower to accept another Caldwell in Kelly's life, but now he too was on the way to becoming a friend.

"Did you call Nick?" The question broke into her pleasant memories.

"Yes." Kelly's smile grew more determined, even as the corners of her mouth trembled with the effort. She would miss Nick, her friend, her mentor, her source of security. He had been gruff today, and she knew it had been to hide his own sadness. "Yes, I spoke to Nick. He wished us luck."

"And he meant it."

"I know." Kelly said no more, a lost look on her face. Though he ached to stop the car and take her in his arms to comfort her, Jake allowed her this private moment to say a silent good-bye to those she loved.

By the time he wheeled the car into the loading zone in back of one of the city's most fashionable and exclusive stores, she was back in control. A small smile hovered again on her lips.

"Better?" In only a word he told her he understood and cared.

"Much, thank you." And the last of her sadness was hidden away.

They had spent the morning at this store choosing clothing and accessories. When she had balked at either quantity or price, Jake simply ignored her objections. Despite her concern, Kelly had enjoyed watching him turn on the full force of his charm, insuring that needed alterations would be done immediately.

"She never had a chance," Kelly murmured.

"Did you say something, love?"

She laughed. "I said that poor clerk never had a chance. You had her charmed out of her socks inside of five minutes. If you had asked for the first brick in the foundation, she would've turned the building over."

"Guilty as charged." Jake grinned, refusing to be daunted. "But it got results, didn't it? You sit tight. I'll be back in a jiffy, then we'll be on our way."

When he returned, he wasn't alone. Two young men accompanied him, carrying stacks of boxes that were wrapped in heavy silver paper bearing the unicorn symbol of the store.

"Jake!" Kelly gasped as they placed package after package in the backseat. "What on earth is all this? We didn't buy this much. There must be some mistake."

"No mistake," he answered blithely. He tipped the men and slid back into the car. "I added a few extra things I thought you might need."

"What things? You've already bought more than I could ever use."

"Ahhh, Kelly, what shopping trip is ever complete without some surprises? When we get to the island you can see for yourself what I bought, and maybe even model a few things." He smiled mischievously as he maneuvered the car smoothly into the flow of traffic.

Kelly realized she was seeing another side of his personality. The solemn, aloof man who had watched her across a smoky room had been transformed into one who laughed and teased. One who planned surprises for her with almost boyish glee. He had come forcefully into her life, and with his determination had given her back hope for a better tomorrow. Her gaze lingered on his strong profile as she wondered at his willingness to accept the burden of his brother's tragic irresponsibility.

A sudden need to touch him made her tremble. She wanted to know the crispness of his hair and the warmth of his skin. But even as the need was born, she fought desperately to suppress it. Looking away quickly, she curled her hands into tight, painful fists and cursed herself for an idiot. She mustn't allow herself to lose sight of the truth of this arrangement, or the reason for his kindness. He was gentle and caring, but she must never forget it was for the sake of the child. His brother's child.

"Kelly, you're frowning. Is something wrong, don't you feel well?" His words were bittersweet to her as she wished his concern was truly for her.

"I'm fine. In fact, I don't have a care in the world," she lied. "We pregnant ladies are moody. It's our prerogative, you know. So if I frown occasionally, just ignore me."

"You're a little hard to ignore. I'd rather see you smile, because I've fallen in love with your dimple."

She laughed, even as her heart contracted at his soft rejoinder. He was only joking. She must remember! She must never let down her guard and act the fool. Once was enough. What was it about these Caldwell men that she found so attractive? One she had wanted to protect, the other she simply wanted.

"Oh, no!" Horrified by the implications of her thoughts, she was totally unaware that she had spoken aloud.

"Kelly!" Jake hurriedly pulled the car to the side

of the road. "You're pale as a ghost." He drew her into his arms, one hand pressing her head to his chest.

Kelly was drowning in the heady scent of him. Here, in this man's arms, was where she wanted to be. An ugly shame filled her. What kind of woman was she? Pregnant with another man's child and wanting *this* man. She, who had never known true desire, was reveling in his touch.

"You're trembling." Jake's breath was warm on her cheek. "Are you ill? Are you in pain?"

"No, Jake, please let me go." She struggled away from him. "It's just that I suddenly felt car sick." The lie was thick on her tongue.

"Would you like to stop for the night?" He reached to draw her to him, then stopped, remembering that for now she didn't welcome his touch.

"It'll pass. It must have been all the excitement."

"You're worn out and it's my fault," he growled in self-reproach. "We should've waited until tomorrow to leave, but I was so anxious to get away . . . Dammit! We'll stop for the night at the next motel."

"No!" She bolted upright. "I'd rather go on." The guilt of her lie made her more determined not to disrupt his plans.

"Are you sure, Kelly?"

"Positive. I'll just lean back and sleep a bit, then I'll be fine." To prove her point, she touched the button on the control panel in the door and, like magic, her seat reclined.

Jake retrieved his discarded jacket from the back seat. "Here, put this over you so you don't get cold." He gently tucked the soft cashmere around her. Kelly dared not open her eyes for fear he would read the turmoil in them. She barely heard him as he whispered, "Sleep well, sweet Kelly."

She meant only to pretend to sleep, but the roads were smooth and the car comfortable. With the fragrance of his cologne filling her senses, she drifted into sleep. When her ragged breathing slowed and settled into an easy rhythm, Jake relaxed. Her pallor and trembling had frightened him, but more than that, his own reaction had disturbed him.

From the first, Kelly had filled him with conflicting emotions. Anger had warred with pity; then distrust with concern; and now respect for her grief waged full battle with a deep affection and crushing desire that grew with every breath he drew. In an unguarded instant he had forgotten what he couldn't allow himself to forget. Legal or not, in word, thought, and deed, Kelly had been his brother's wife . . . and she carried his child. She loved Scott. It was too soon, her grief too raw, for her to feel anything for him but gratitude. Jake grimaced. Gratitude was the last thing he wanted from Kelly. He wanted more, much more. He must move carefully, give her time to heal, and in the meantime, control his feelings.

He thought of the future, to the times when, for the benefit of others, he must touch her, kiss her. He groaned aloud, feeling already the frustrations he knew would come. Even now as she snuggled in the seat by his side, his body quickened with the desire to touch her. Unconsciously he lifted his hand to stroke her smooth cheek, then jerked guiltily away as she stirred.

"Damn fool!" he cursed under his breath. "Acting like a teenager, mooning over a girl who hardly knows me."

Grimly he concentrated on the long drive to Kiawah, the lovely island that was only a short distance from his Charleston home. In this paradise for lovers, he would spend two weeks with Kelly. As part of their plan, this would be a time of learning about each other and growing comfortable together to make their performance more believable. Living with her day after day, could he contain himself within the bounds of friendship, when even now he wanted to draw her close, to fill his strangely empty arms with her?

Wishing desperately he could shut out his thoughts, he drove hour after hour. Never had the three hundred miles from Atlanta to the island seemed so long. As the miles sped by, Kelly didn't stir. Knowing she needed the rest, he drove with even greater care. His eyes often strayed to her, and he felt a mixture of tenderness, concern, and regret. Midnight was long past by the time he drove through the guarded gates of the island. At the end of a winding street, Jake stopped the car before a small but lovely gray shingled cottage that sat a bit apart from the other beachfront homes.

"Kelly, we're home." He touched her lightly to wake her. She stirred and opened her eyes, but seemed still half-asleep. He led her up the steps and inside, then returned to the car for their things. He helped her to dress for bed, sternly repressing his response to her beauty. She was asleep again before he left the room.

A soft murmur filled the room as sunlight slanted through the louvered french doors. Still groggy with sleep, Kelly drifted dreamily on the soothing sound. It was as restful as the quiet hush of the wind in the pines or the hypnotic song of the—

"The sea!" Kelly tossed back the covers. Heedless of her bare feet and filmy nightgown, she flew to the doors, impatiently unlatching them and throwing them open.

On the small balcony outside her bedroom, she watched the sunlight glint off the water. It was a mild October day, more like late summer than early fall. A warm breeze danced from sea to shore, teasing the few sunbathers and joggers on the beach. In all her twenty-five years, Kelly had never seen the sea. She had dreamed of it, seen pictures of it, but never in her wildest imaginings had she expected to be standing before it, taking in its beauty, being caressed by its breeze. The sound of the surf was a lovely melody.

"Good morning." The quiet voice at her side startled her. She turned to find Jake, her robe in his hand.

"Good morning, Jake." A laugh bubbled from her lips. "Isn't it a beautiful day?"

"Beautiful," he agreed, but his eyes were only for her.

"Ohhh!" Kelly's hand flew to her cheek as a blush stained her face. All her ancient and threadbare gowns had been tossed emphatically into a trash bin by Jake. His choice, this silken creation she was wearing now, clung lovingly to every curve, revealing what the sheer fabric pretended to hide. "I didn't think . . . I . . ."

"Shhh, never mind, sweetheart. It's a little late for modesty, since I was the one who dressed you for bed." A wicked grin lifted the corners of his mouth, even as he feasted on the shadowed loveliness of her breasts. "Here, put this on. I love the view, but I'd prefer not to share it."

He helped the mortified Kelly slip into the robe. She stubbornly refused to meet his eyes or to speak. And just as stubbornly refused to admit to herself her body's obvious response to the implication of his words and the all too male look in his eyes. She stared helplessly at the sea.

"You find the sea intriguing?" His low voice caressed her ears.

"It's enchanting. Waking to its sound was beautiful. I think I could stand here forever, listening to its whisper." In her confusion, her words were more poetic than she intended. He chuckled at her eloquence and she blushed again.

"Why don't we have our breakfast here on the balcony?" he said. "Sea air is good for the appetite and you, my dear lady, need to eat more."

"I'd like that, and what you say must be true. I'm starved."

"Then, your wish is my command." He bowed low, a twinkle in his eyes. "I just *happen* to have a tray ready for *just* such an occasion."

Kelly laughed as she curtsied and took the seat he offered. Jake produced a tray filled to overflowing, then sat beside her and they both ate enthusiastically.

"I can't eat another bite," Kelly moaned as she

leaned back in her chair. "At this rate, I'll be waddling soon instead of walking."

"Some extra weight can't hurt you, but we don't want to overdo it. If you'll put on something a bit less provocative, I'll take you for a walk on the beach." His grin was positively wicked as his gaze swept the elegant robe Kelly had tucked firmly about her. She wasn't aware that each of her self-conscious tugs emphasized even more what the sunlit threads embraced.

"I'd love to go for a walk, but first I'd like to sort through my new wardrobe. Everything was so lovely."

"I was beginning to think you'd forgotten."

"Jake!" She grew contrite, her light mood suddenly somber. "I could never forget how kind you've been to me. Never!"

"Sweetheart, I was only teasing." He covered her hand with his. "It's easy to be kind to you. It's no more than you deserve and it's fun. Now, you get dressed while I clear this away, then we'll open the packages."

Later, Kelly sat spellbound on the floor amid a mountain of boxes. Scattered throughout the room, across chairs and over the bed, were garments of all colors and descriptions. Jake watched her with an amused smile. She was like a child at Christmas.

In his surprise packages she found frothy, delicate undergarments; a very simple but elegant dinner dress; a hostess gown of the softest silk; and bracelets, necklaces, and earrings to complement both.

Finally, there was only one box left. Kelly tore off the paper and lifted the lid. Nestled among the tissue like a jewel was a negligee and robe of burnished gold, trimmed with a beige gossamerlike lace.

"This is the most beautiful thing I've ever seen." She lifted it reverently from the box, stroking the shimmering fabric with a loving hand.

"It reminded me of your hair," Jake said, his voice unaccountably husky.

When she looked up at him her eyes, shimmering with happiness, were as lovely and as burnished gold as the gown. "How can I ever thank you?"

"A wifely kiss would suffice." He smiled as he opened his arms.

Without thought, Kelly launched herself into his waiting embrace. The kiss she pressed to his mouth was intended to be light, but in its gaiety it somehow went awry. The velvet softness of her mouth met his with an unplanned urgency. Her sheer delight was there in the fervent caress of her lips. First stunned, then entranced beyond measure, Jake closed his arms about her and drew her onto his knees. Cradling her tenderly against him, discretion fell before the sweet, wild soaring of his need. Slowly, hungrily, his kiss deepened, shattering all reason as his mouth ravished hers. With a gentle yielding, she accepted the first seeking caress of his tongue, rejoicing in its thorough exploration. As her fingers burrowed into the unruly waves of his hair, his shaking hand slid from her arm to her side, then moved lovingly over her midriff toward her breast. He yearned to cup its fullness in his palm, to seek with his lips the tautening peak that promised delight. Then his arm brushed over the swell of her abdomen, shattering beyond recall the enchantment of the moment. He drew away abruptly, cursing violently, shocked back into cold sanity by her pregnancy.

"Damn! Kelly, forgive me. I didn't mean for that to happen." Unsteadily he put her from him, his eyes not meeting hers.

"Jake . . . I . . ." Kelly faltered, her body trembling, her heart stricken by what she had done. Like a fool she had thrown herself at him and had enticed him to respond. That bright flicker of joy that had lit within her died with shame. He must surely find her disgusting. When their gazes collided, she searched his face anxiously, but could read nothing in his carefully controlled expression. He was being kind, pretending that she hadn't been so ludicrous. "I'm sorry. I didn't mean—"

"Shhh." His finger against her lips stopped her stumbling words. "Let's forget it happened. Mark it down as a mistake we both made."

"But I—"

"Hush, Kelly." He tapped her gently on her upturned nose. "Help me clear this away and we'll take that walk."

They worked silently, each lost in private thoughts, each in their separateness remembering the beauty of what could not be again. They worked efficiently and in little time the room was in order. As she hung the last of the clothing away, he finished with the boxes.

"Will you be warm enough in that?" he asked, nodding at the gold velour jogging suit she had put on. The kiss might never have been.

"It's fine. Jake?" She hesitated. "I do thank you for all you've done."

"No more thanks needed." He spoke curtly, then cursed himself as a shadow of pain crossed her face. With an effort he brightened his tone. "Come on, Sunshine, let's go get some exercise."

With a deliberate casualness, he draped his arm about her shoulders, and led her from the house onto the snowy white beach. The light breeze lifted and tossed her curls, giving her the tousled look of a child. At first she walked sedately by him, then her delight in the sea overcame her reticence. Somewhat uncertain, she wandered from his side to the water's edge. She stepped forward, following the ebb of a wave, then dashed madly back to dry sand, her laughter drifting in the salty air.

"Careful," Jake called as she began to play a game of chase with each new wave that lapped softly at the shore, her dancing steps leaving pretty tracks in the moist sand. He watched her fondly, deeply pleased with her laughter and her joy.

"Look!" She drew a round shell from the water. "It's beautiful." She offered her treasure for him to admire.

"That's an old shell, washed up on shore a long time ago." He took it from her. "It's broken and ugly and almost worn smooth from tumbling in the surf. There are newer, prettier shells all along the beach, and live ones just beyond the water's edge. When it's warmer, I'll show you how to find them."

"I'd like to keep this one," she said quietly. "It's my first seashell ever."

Surprised again at her pleasure in the simplest of things, he smiled warmly. "Sweetheart, you can keep all the shells you can find. Wait here. I'll go get a bag, then we'll have a serious shell hunt."

He was off before she could say anything. She watched his retreating back, admiring, not for the first time, the play of light on the sun-streaked depths of his hair. The ripple of brawny muscles beneath his knit shirt was beautiful. As was the suppleness of his narrow hips encased in soft, ancient denim. Long, lean, and breathtaking, he towered over her by nearly a foot, but never intimidated her. He was a marvelous man, making even their bizarre relationship pleasant. A smile played over her lips as he started running across the sand with the athletic grace he decried. He would laugh if she told him she thought he was magnificent.

For over an hour, they wandered along the shoreline and their bag of treasures grew. No shell was too small nor too plain for Kelly. Jake kept a constant watch for signs that she was tiring, but her enthusiasm never flagged. When he called a halt to the excursion, her face fell, but only until he promised they would walk the next day in the opposite direction.

As they strolled hand in hand back to the house, Jake was delighted with the healthy glow in her cheeks and the new quickness in her step. The late October sun had touched her face with faint color. A few more days on the beach and she would look the picture of rosy good health. Everything would be perfect but for his nagging worry about the smallness of her pregnancy.

"Kelly?"

"Hmmm?" She didn't raise her head, for even

now she searched the sand for one more shell to add to her collection.

"I'd like to make an appointment for you to see an obstetrician in Charleston as soon as possible."

"I'll need to find a doctor, but there's no rush. I'm fine, you know."

"For my own peace of mind, I'd like you to see a friend of mine. Soon."

"All right, Jake, if it will reassure you."

"It will."

"Then I'll go whenever you say."

"I'll give him a call later tonight." He smiled at her with a new brilliance and an easier mind.

After their walk and at his insistence she agreed to take a nap, but not before her shells were lined up along the railing of the balcony. She made one last attempt to persuade him that she wasn't tired and didn't need to rest, but he wouldn't listen.

"You don't realize yet how tiring walking in the sand can be. Just lie down for a few minutes. If you can't sleep, then at least rest."

"Okay," she grumbled. "But only because you insist. Remember, I told you I wouldn't be able to sleep."

Kelly did mean only to rest, but the soothing sounds of the surf lulled her into a deep and restful sleep. Aware that her faint rustlings had stopped, Jake tiptoed into the room. Chuckling to himself, he covered her with a light blanket, then carefully flicked a grain of sand from the hand that curled against her cheek. Seeing her as she was now, he found himself wishing fiercely that the baby would be a girl who looked exactly like Kelly . . . and that the baby were his.

His expression grew bleak. Though he didn't understand the strong feelings Kelly fostered in him, he lived in dread that he would lose her. "No!" he whispered. Looking hungrily at the sleeping woman, his chest rose and fell in a deep, shuddering breath before he turned away and left the room.

Kelly slept for three hours and woke wonderfully

refreshed. Since it was too late for lunch, they decided to have an early dinner, then walk again on the beach in the moonlight.

"Remember, Kelly," Jake cautioned firmly. "We'll only go if it's not too cool."

She merely smiled and continued to tear the lettuce for the salad as she planned the walk she *would* take later. Unsuspecting, Jake again set the table on the balcony, because it pleased Kelly. There by the flickering candlelight, protected by a hurricane globe, he plied her with chilled shrimp, fresh fruit, and the light green salad.

"Please, Jake, no more." Kelly rested her hand on her middle. "I'm stuffed. It's delicious, but I can't eat another bite."

"Not even a brownie?"

"You're a wicked man, Jason Caldwell. How could you tempt me so? Someone must have told you chocolate is my weakness. My only weakness, mind you." She laughed as she wagged a finger at him.

"Kathleen's the culprit," Jake defended himself. "She sent them with us."

"Let's have our walk, then maybe I can find room for one small brownie."

Jake knew he'd been outmaneuvered and his laughter filled the air. It was a happy sound, one she loved. "You win, Sunshine. Go get your jacket. I'll stick these in the dishwasher before we leave."

The night air was balmy as they trudged arm in arm across the hard-packed sand. The tide was out, the beach wide and deserted. The sky was so clear that the stars seemed to glow more brilliantly than ever.

"My goodness," Kelly exclaimed. "The stars look close enough to reach out and touch."

Jake only smiled and led her carefully around a large piece of driftwood. Kelly didn't see it, for her eyes were directed toward the sky with the same intensity with which she had watched the sand earlier. The teasing breeze of the morning had turned into a chilly harder blowing wind. He lay a comforting arm about her shoulders and drew her close to his body. For a short distance they walked in silence, neither needing to speak.

"Jake?" Kelly said suddenly.

"Yep?"

"Why do you call me Sunshine?"

"Lots of reasons." His pace didn't change, and when Kelly thought he would say no more, he spoke quietly into the starlit night. "Maybe it's because your hair is like the morning sun, and when you're happy you sparkle like a ray of light. But mostly I think it's because of your smile. It has the warmth of the summer sun. I can't explain it any better than that." He shrugged. "To me you are sunshine."

Kelly stopped abruptly. A moonbeam turned to diamonds the unshed tears in her eyes. "That's the most beautiful thing I've ever heard. No one's ever said anything half so nice to me before."

"No one?"

Wordlessly she shook her head, finding speech impossible.

"Then Scott was a bigger fool than I realized," he growled, drawing her back to him.

"But you don't understand about Scott!"

"No! I don't want to hear about him, Kelly. This is our time. We have these weeks together to learn about each other. Forget Scott. There's only the two of us and the baby to think about now." With his handkerchief he patted away the tears that had started to flow. When she rewarded him with a tremulous smile, he kissed her lightly and hugged her, his palm cradling her cheek for a fleeting instant before he released her. "That's better. Now smile so I can see your dimples."

In the next few days a pattern emerged. They walked the beach both morning and night. In the afternoon it became a ritual that she would suggest skipping the rest period, while Jake would insist with mock severity that she not. The days flew past. The best part for both were the evenings spent in deep, fascinating conversation, learning about each other.

"Kelly," Jake said as he draped her shawl about her shoulders, his fingers brushing across the nape of her neck in a whisper of a caress, "are you sure this will be warm enough?"

"I'm sure." She unconsciously stroked his knuckles with her chin. His breathing faltered and his fingers convulsively curved into her tender flesh. Puzzled, Kelly looked into his rugged face, but could read nothing there. Their gazes met and held, yet still she couldn't see beyond his kind concern for her comfort. She moistened her dry lips with the tip of her tongue. "I'll be fine. Thank you for the shawl."

Drawing his hand away slowly, he sat down beside her. Their chairs were pulled close to the balcony railing where Kelly liked to sit each evening and watch the sunset. She was always enchanted by the changing sea and sky, as the yellow and blue of day turned to fiery reds and oranges, then a soft purple that marked the end of light.

"It's strange you've never seen the sea before," Jake said softly, noting the radiance of her expression.

"Not so strange," she countered with a slight shake of her head. "There was never the time, nor the money."

"Tell me what your childhood was like, Kelly." He leaned back and waited.

"It's not a very interesting story," she said finally. "I'm sure we could find something better to talk about."

"I'd like to know," he persisted gently.

Kelly turned to face him, trying to understand what was in his eyes. As he leaned back in the shadowed recesses of the balcony, she could see only the strong, clean lines of his profile. He lifted a cigarette to his lips, one of the few she'd ever seen him smoke. She waited in gathering moonlight, wondering where to begin.

"It's funny," she said, laughing ruefully. "There's really very little to tell, but I don't know where to begin."

"Is your mother still living?"

"I don't know." Though she tried to mask it, the hurt was still there. "She left me with Aunt Emily when I was six years old. She came around some after that, but gradually we saw less and less of her until finally, she stopped coming."

"How long were you with your aunt?"

"She died when I was eighteen. She was a wonderful woman. If it hadn't been for her, I would probably have been sent to a foster home."

"Were you happy with her?"

"Yes, except that she was so old. I felt guilty for being such a burden. She was my grandmother's sister, you know."

Jake nodded. "What did you do after she died?"

"My life really didn't change much." Kelly's voice was low and carefully steady. "A little lonelier, but no different."

Jake watched the darkness lift from her face as the moon began to rise. Even as she spoke of a life of loss and loneliness, there was no self-pity, only remembered sadness. He could see the strength and courage that had made the lonely eighteen-year-old girl the woman she had become. Jake stirred restlessly as a strange tightness closed about his throat.

"With the money from the sale of the house she left me, I had enough to put myself through college if I worked and planned very carefully," Kelly continued almost absently.

"In Nick's neighborhood, it couldn't have sold for much."

"No," she agreed softly, her eyes again on the water that was sparkling like dancing diamonds in the moonlight. "But it was a start. Nick let me play the piano, and with my salary from that and an apartment in the low-rent district, I managed."

"I can't see how." The tightness had grown as he felt a choking rage at the hardships she had fought. His voice sank to a deep, husky rumble. "It must have been hard, a girl alone, trying to juggle a career and attend classes."

She laughed. "You flatter me. It was hardly a career. Nick easily could have gotten a better piano player."

"Technically, perhaps, but none with your warmth, nor with your flair for putting your heart into the music."

"Now you really do flatter me, but thank you." Kelly leaned further back into the mauve and green cushions of the rattan chair, listening to the hushed sounds of the surf as it tumbled over the sand. "I had a good life, Jake. We weren't rich by any means, but we had what we needed. Aunt Emily more than made up for my mother's constant absences, and I've had some good friends. Friends like Nick and Mike and Kathleen."

"But they're so much older. Weren't there any friends your own age? Girlfriends?" His voice took on a teasing note. "And surely, you had the expected number of boyfriends under foot."

"N-no." She shook her head, faltering for the first time. "There was no one until Scott."

Jake stirred and rose abruptly. "It's late. Time you had that glass of milk you promised to drink before bedtime."

Kelly tried again to read his mood, but could see nothing in his face. Slowly she took his extended hand and rose gracefully, allowing him to lead her inside.

She had drunk the prescribed glass of milk and had just slipped into bed when Jake tapped on her door. "Could we talk for one more minute, Kelly?"

"Of course, come in." She sat up in bed, adjusting the pillows behind her back as he sat beside her.

"Would you mind if we cut our stay here short?" he said. "There are some things in Charleston that need my attention and I'd like for you to see the doctor."

"I don't mind," she answered gravely. "We can leave whenever you wish. I should have realized that you were taking valuable time away from your work. I shouldn't have been so selfish."

"You could never be selfish. I don't think you know how." He took her hand in his, his thumb caressing her knuckles. "Get a good night's sleep. We still have tomorrow and we'll make it a special day. How about a picnic? We could find a nice, quiet spot just for the two of us."

"I'd like that," she murmured drowsily. She was tired, but it was a pleasant tiredness, not the bone weary, aching fatigue she'd known in Atlanta.

Jake sat silently as her eyelids drooped once, twice, then for the last time. With a gentle hand, he tucked the sheet beneath her chin and brushed back her curls. "Sleep well, Kelly. You don't have to fight the world anymore. I'm here."

Kelly sensed more than knew when he rose. For a fleeting instant she thought she felt the warm, vibrant brush of his mouth against her forehead. As the door closed softly behind him, her last waking thought was that once again he had refused to let her speak of Scott.

Five

Their last day on the island dawned clear, bright, and even warmer than usual. Kelly was standing on her balcony when Jake came to wake her.

"You're an early bird this morning," he teased in his soft drawl.

As he joined her in the sunlight, she could see droplets of water glistening in his hair. He had taken a shower and, as usual, had fought his natural curl by severely slicking back the soaked strands. Stubbornly, as it dried, the hair was springing back into a subdued wave. Later, as it ruffled in the wind, it would begin to wave even more. Kelly longed to bury her fingers in the crisp hair, to tousle it, turning it into the halo of curls she knew it would be. He was a handsome man, saved from real beauty by the ruggedness of his features. What would it be like to cradle his head in her hands as she drew his mouth to hers? Dismayed by her wayward thoughts, she turned quickly away, her eyes focused on the ever changing sea.

"I've been up for hours," she said. If he noticed the huskiness in her voice, he made no comment. "I couldn't sleep late on our last day here. I'll never forget this week." She didn't know that the wistful look she gave him almost unmanned him, nearly destroying his resolve not to take her into his hungry arms.

"You can always come back, Kelly. As often as you like. It's less than an hour's drive from our home. You could easily come for the day."

"I'd like that."

"It would be good for you to take walks here while

I'm at the office. The exercise would build up your appetite."

"Build up my appetite! Good heavens, Jake, if I ate much more I'd explode."

"But you're so little."

"Oh, Jake." She shook her head ruefully, an indulgent grin on her face. "When will you ever believe that I'm perfectly all right?"

"You're too small," he insisted stubbornly. "It's not natural."

"Okay, if it will make you feel better, I'll come here often. I'll walk and then I'll eat until you beg me to stop. How much would you like? Two or three hundred pounds?"

"This isn't a laughing matter, Kelly. I'm sorry if my concern amuses you."

For the first time, Kelly realized how deep-seated his concerns were. She had forgotten that she was his only link with the brother he had lost. Her child would, in a small way, be the perpetuation of Scott. Contritely, she touched his arm, hoping to mend the breach. Her heart twisted when he flinched away, his face dark and brooding.

"Don't be angry, Jake. I'm sorry I teased. From now on I'll try not to worry you. I'll come out here every day I can."

"Promise me that you won't come alone. Bring Mother or Lydia with you."

"I wouldn't want to interrupt their schedule. I could come alone just as easily."

"No. Not alone. Promise me, Kelly."

"You're being foolish, Jake. I can take care—"

"Promise." It was a gentle plea, laced with steel.

"If it will make you feel better, I promise."

"It will." His voice was soft now, almost a caress. "Thank you."

Kelly laughed, realizing that this time it was she had who had been outmaneuvered. "You devious rascal."

As she looked up at him, her laughter stopped as quickly as it had begun. There was something in his eyes, something unsettling, something that she would give her soul to understand. Could it be tenderness? Kelly realized, with a start, that she was staring at him like an infatuated girl. She turned away, hoping to hide the betraying blush that rose in her cheeks. Her fingers clutched a shell she had set out and she nervously traced its contours.

"You love the sea more than anyone I've ever seen."

"It's exciting." She left unsaid that even the sea would never be so exciting without him.

He chuckled as he tucked a curl behind her ear. "Hurry and dress. We've a busy day. Breakfast at the Jasmine Porch first, and then the Straw Market. I guarantee that you'll like both."

Jake was right. She was captivated by the inn and the market. She raptly watched the weaving of the sweet grass and was awed by the delicate baskets. Jake delighted her when he insisted that she choose one for herself, and for his mother and Lydia.

"Now what would you like to do?" he asked after stowing her purchases in the car. "Would you like to walk on the beach or would you like to see some more of the island?"

"The island," she said promptly. "I'd like to see if it's all this lovely."

"The island it shall be, then."

The remainder of the morning and part of the afternoon was spent in exploring every part of Kiawah. Jake drove slowly along the winding roads, finding new delight in familiar things as he saw them through Kelly's eyes. Promptly at one, when he decided that Kelly was hungry, they stopped at a quiet, secluded lake. On a blanket spread under the branches of an ancient, gnarled oak, they feasted on the food they had brought with them. When the picnic basket had been repacked, they lay quietly side by side, content.

Sunlight danced brightly over rustling leaves and Kelly's drowsy mind wandered to days filled with warmth and laughter. Not since childhood had she been so carefree. Teaching her that troubles shared were easier to bear, Jake had willingly shouldered her problems. With unfailing kindness, he had lavished her with care, teasing and laughing as she bloomed with a newfound peace.

Stealing the rare pleasure of looking at him unobserved, she studied his face, lingering long on the thick fringe of gold-tipped lashes that curled slightly as they lay against his cheeks. He didn't move. Only the blade of grass between his lips swayed as he lay with his arms behind his head. Intent on her delightful exploration, she wasn't aware that glittering eyes watched her behind that curtain of lashes. Nor that his breathing quickened as in a beguiling blend of seductive innocence, she stroked his lips lightly with the tip of an inquisitive finger. The impish grin that curved her own lips was lost in a startled cry when she suddenly found herself flat on her back.

"So you want to play, do you?" Jake growled in mock ferocity. "Then shall we play this game?" He teased her with kisses softer than a whisper, stroking and caressing with sensual expertise until her lips parted willingly, awaiting a total possession that never came. Instead, he drew away slowly.

"Have you no idea how irresistible you are?" he murmured. A strange smile quirked his lips as his fingers tangled in her hair. "Perhaps it's fortunate for the so-called stronger sex that you don't," he added with a laugh as he rolled away. His manner had been light, but a deadly earnestness had surfaced for an intriguing instant, leaving Kelly puzzled and confused.

He lay as he had before, utterly still with that peculiar, loose-limbed grace, his arm thrown over his eyes. Kelly measured the deep, even rise and fall of his chest. Calm, composed, the happy teasing with that peculiar underlying fierceness forgotten. Indeed, had it ever existed except in her fanciful anticipations? He had awakened in her strange and delicious sensations as a new world opened to her. He had called her innocent and she was, incredibly so. Though she carried a child, it was the child of loneliness. Kelly knew nothing of the consuming passions of love, and recognized it neither in her own stirring emotions, nor in the eyes of the man who watched her while feigning calmness.

Nervously she waited for him to speak, reminding herself that he had only been teasing. Pressing her icy hands to her face, she tried desperately to divert her mind from her foolish response and seized on a worrisome thought.

"Would you tell me about your family?" she said. "Maybe I wouldn't be so frightened tomorrow if I knew what to expect."

"There's no need to be frightened, Kelly." He rolled to his side and leaned his head on his hand. "Only three people need concern you and you'll like them. There's not a single dragon who lives in the castle."

"Tell me, please," she persisted.

"All right. First there's Mother. She really defies description. She's little, redheaded, and with a fiery temper to match. Other than her family, her one passion is flowers. Lydia is both fair and dark, and the gentlest person I've ever met." Jake hesitated. "She's been in a wheelchair for two years now."

Kelly gasped. "What happened?"

He stared blankly into the distance. "I don't know exactly. I always figured there was more to it than either of them told me. Lydia and Scott were driving home one evening and another car hit them. Scott's injuries were minor. Lydia's legs were broken and she'll never walk again."

Kelly didn't know what to say, what she could say, so she remained silent and waited for the bleakness to leave Jake's eyes.

"Lydia's wonderful," he finally said. "I'm sure you'll enjoy her company." He smiled. "And last, but certainly not least, there's Monroe."

"Monroe?"

"He's the butler, but that's simply a title. He's

truly more a member of the family than a servant. Wherever Mother is, he's always just a step behind." His hand cupped Kelly's chin. "You needn't worry. They're nice people and if anything should go wrong, I'll be there."

His promise of support warmed her. "Thank you, Jake. I'll try not to let you down."

"I know." He was quiet for a long time, watching Kelly as she gazed over the rippling waters of the nearby lake. "Are we clear on the sequences of our story?"

"I think so." She sat up straighter, folding her arms about her knees, toying with the chain at her neck. "Scott and I were—"

"Not Scott!" The words exploded from him with an unexpected violence as he sat up. Startled, Kelly stared at him, puzzled by his reaction. Then she realized what she had said.

"I'm sorry," she whispered.

"Kelly," he said gently, his anger gone. "We can't afford a slip like that. You must be careful. So many people would be hurt if either of us make a wrong move. Please try. For me?"

She straightened her shoulders even more, paused, gathering her strength, and began again. "Last December when your mother was ill, you spent three weeks looking for Scott. You met me the first week. We married impulsively, almost immediately, then quarreled and parted. Because of your mother's illness you never told her. In March we met again and I became pregnant. And now, because of the baby, we've decided to try again. We've always been deeply in love . . ." She faltered, clenching her hands tightly. "That never . . ." She ran her hands through her windblown hair in despair. "Jake, no one's going to believe this. I can't remember the dates and I'm not very good at lying. Just let me go away. No one can be hurt if they never know about the baby. I'd never tell them, I swear."

"Hush." He gathered her shivering body close to his. "You don't have to remember the exact dates in

March. I was away more than I was home, so no one can pin us down on that. And"—he turned her face up to his—"there are others to consider, not just my family. There's you and the baby, have you forgotten? She'll bear the name Caldwell and we'll be proud of her. There'll be no slinking off into hidden corners, living lonely lives on the dark fringes. She'll grow up warm and secure, surrounded by a loving family. I won't let anyone, not Mother, not Lydia, and especially not you, be hurt anymore. And I won't let this baby's life be tainted by the mistakes of an irresponsible man. She'll be *my* daughter."

"Your *daughter*?" Her voice quavered anew.

"Yes, my daughter."

"Has it crossed your mind that this daughter might be a son?"

"Nope. It's out of the question. I've placed my order for a daughter." She smiled as he had intended she should and he smiled in return. "Now, continue."

Kelly drew strength from his encouraging smile and her voice was firmer, more confident. "We've reconciled again, this time for good. We're very much in love and always have been, despite our differences. Now, with great delight, we await the birth of our . . . daughter."

"Perfect! I knew you could get through the story." He kissed her forehead gently, holding her close. With her head pressed to his chest, his heart beating against her ear, Kelly could feel a strange tension building within him.

"There is one more thing." His words were hesitant and grave. "There's been another woman. It was nothing, and she'll be discreet. It's just that . . . Well, dammit! I'd never commit adultery . . . at least not knowingly . . . I . . ."

Kelly pulled out of his embrace and faced him. "Jake, I understand." She touched his shoulder with a soothing hand. "It wouldn't truly be adultery anyway. It isn't something that's going to bother me."

"The past is beyond my control, but I can promise you there'll be no one else."

"I can't ask that of you!"

"Yes, you can, Kelly. You're my wife now, and you can ask for fidelity." He smiled at her. "Besides, no one in his right mind would cheat on you."

Kelly's face flamed at his allusion to her untried passion. His smile faded and she knew there was something more. Patiently, she waited until he spoke again.

"There's more, sweetheart." He stroked her cheek with a single finger, never taking his eyes from hers. "If we're to be convincing, we'll have to share the same room . . . and bed."

"Oh, no!" She pulled further away from him, startled by his words.

"I'm sorry, but there's no other way."

For a long time she sat very still, moving only to brush her hair from her face. He could see she was turning the thought over in her mind, weighing every aspect. "You're right, of course," she murmured. "If we're to make everyone believe we're wildly in love there's no choice but to share the same room."

"And bed?"

"Yes."

"I'll have to play the lover as well as I know how in public, but I'll not take the role into the bedroom. I'll hold you and kiss you at times, but never when we're alone." Jake paused, his face unreadable, then almost inaudibly murmured, "Unless you should want me to."

"I understand what you must do," she said, smiling, ignoring the uncontrollable spark of desire his last words had ignited.

"It would help if you would play the lover with me. Touch me and look at me with that soft smile of yours. Seek me out. Show those who watch that you love me." He looked at her steadily, gauging the effect of his words, leaving Kelly to wonder what it was he wanted of her.

"I'll do my best. I've never been much of an actress, but I will try." In her heart, Kelly had begun to realize that she could do all the things he was asking without acting. Just the thought of playing the lover for Jake set her mind awhirl.

By the time he had her seated comfortably in the car, Kelly had regained her composure. She expressed one last desire to take the Jeep Safari, an excursion into the interior of the island, but Jake said adamantly that the ride was too rugged for her in her condition. She accepted his judgment gracefully and in exchange for her promise to rest for the remainder of the day, he planned an evening of dining and dancing at the Inn.

Well rested from her nap, Kelly had dressed with care, determined that this night would be one she would never forget. At a secluded table, she and Jake talked and laughed. He seemed to touch her all the time. Whenever her hand rested on the table, he stroked her knuckles, enfolding her hand in his. When she had smeared a bit of shrimp sauce on her lips, with provocative care he had blotted it away with his white linen napkin. Once, in the sheer exuberance of their festive mood, he had kissed her, softly and gently, on her suddenly trembling lips. Hardly aware of those about them, they were lost in each other until a strident, falsely hearty voice intruded.

"Well, well, well, Jake Caldwell. I haven't seen you here in months." The man who spoke might have been addressing Jake, but his avid gaze was for Kelly alone. "And who might this lovely lady be?"

Jake stood up and offered his hand to the bluff man. "Hello, Howard. I'd like you to meet my wife, Kelly. Kelly, this is Howard Norris."

"How do you do, Mr. Norris?" Kelly timidly offered her hand and found it engulfed in a hamlike fist.

"Jake, you old son of a gun! I didn't know you were married. When was the happy event?" The piercing eyes had not missed the slight swell of her pregnancy.

"You hadn't heard?" Jake's southern drawl, never very pronounced, was now somehow deadly, but the obtuse intruder didn't notice. "You must be slipping, Howard. I thought you always knew everything that happened here or in Charleston. Kelly and I were married in Atlanta last December, weren't we, darling?" Jake traced the line of her jaw with his thumb.

Kelly tilted her head into the palm of his hand. Ignoring the pounding of her foolish heart, she played for the first time the role that was actually the truth. Her lips brushed lightly against his fingers and the eyes she lifted to his were filled with love for all the world to see. Her mouth moved against his skin and her voice was little more than a husky murmur. "Yes, that's right. But it seems like only last week that we met."

Jake's breath caught in his throat. Then at a curious sound from Howard, he relaxed. As he turned away from Kelly, his eyelid drooped in the slightest of winks. Only she knew how hard he was trying not to laugh.

"Won't you join us, Howard?" Jake said.

"Now, Jake. You know I don't like to intrude. Besides, if I had a little girl who looked at me the way this lady looks at you, I'd want to keep her all to myself. But I'll take a rain check."

With a carefree wave, Howard moved on, and Jake sat again. He lifted Kelly's cold hand to his lips. As he kissed her fingertips, he whispered devilishly, "You, sweet Kelly, have just fooled the most notorious gossip in all of Charleston."

Their laughter drew the attention of the other late evening diners. But all they could see was a handsome man holding the hand of the beautiful woman he loved.

"Do I look all right?"

"Yes, Kelly."

"Are you sure my shoes are all right?"

"Yes, Kelly."

"Is my hair mussed?"

"No, Kelly."

"Are you sure my lipstick isn't smeared?"

"Yes, Kelly."

"Will you be ashamed of me?"

There was a screech of brakes as Jake stopped short in the street. He hadn't bothered to signal or pull to the curb. He turned to Kelly impatiently, a wicked gleam in his eyes.

"Jake! You can't just stop in the middle of the street like this. It's illegal. Jake! What're you doing?"

"This." He plucked her from her seat, drawing her torso hard against his chest. She had no time to protest before his mouth came down on hers. It was the loving kiss of her dreams, soft, insistent, urgent. His fingers crept into her hair to cradle her head, his tongue stroked the velvet curve of her lips. Sweetly, without thought, she opened to him. The world retreated; there was nothing save this. Her arms began to slip around his body when the soft, apologetic beep of a horn forced them to part

Reluctantly, Jake released her, his fingers trailing across her shoulders as she slid hurriedly to her seat. She fumbled in her purse for her comb, not daring to meet his eyes as she began to repair the damage.

"Don't." His hand on her arm stopped her.

"My hair—"

"Leave it."

"But—"

"Leave it," he repeated softly. "Your shoes are still all right, but your hair is mussed, your lipstick's smeared, and you look exactly like what you are. A woman who's just been kissed senseless by a man who's crazy about her. And no, I'm not ashamed of you. I never will be."

The horn sounded again, this time a little less apologetic. Jake flashed her a lopsided grin that took her breath away. "So speaks the real world, sweetheart, but maybe we could continue this later?"

This time the horn blared impatiently, rescuing Kelly from the need to reply. She silently blessed the impatient soul, sure he had saved her from babbling like an idiot. She searched again for her comb, not believing for a minute that Jake would want her to meet his family in such disarray.

"Don't." His eyes swept over her, not missing one tumbled curl. "You look like a woman in love. I want them to see you this way. It would be the greatest proof our little charade could have." Satisfied that she would agree, he turned his full attention to managing the twists and turns of the narrow road.

Kelly's heart plummeted. It had been an act. The simple setting of the stage for their first performance. He had been acting and she had forgotten. Like the child who believes that all the tinsel of Christmas is real, she had believed.

Could she survive this? she wondered. Could she play her part then leave when the time came? Yes, she told herself firmly. She could. She must, for the baby. She unconsciously straightened her shoulders, mentally preparing herself for the days and months ahead. She would become the consummate actress, but her role had changed. She would no longer be playing a part for the world; now it was Jake she must convince. He must never suspect that she was not pretending but really in love, a deep love that she sensed would last for as long as she lived.

"Kelly, if you'll look up, you'll see what I consider one of the most beautiful sights in the world."

His words drew her attention from her hands, which were clenched tightly in her lap. Jake slowed the car as they passed through the heavy wrought iron gates with the words CALDWELL HOUSE inscribed on them. Down the long avenue flanked by ancient oaks, she could glimpse a tall, stately mansion, its recessed Palladian portico also framed by oaks. Scattered about the rolling lawn were camellias, azaleas, jasmine, and clusters of fall flowers that bloomed in profusion. Spanish moss had draped itself gracefully over tree limbs and swayed in the wind. It was beautiful.

"Come on, daydreamer, it's time." He had stopped the car and was standing by her side, his hand extended to help her from her seat. "Don't be afraid."

"Jake! Jake!" The heavy front door was flung open. A tiny, colorful figure dashed across the portico, down the walk, and straight into Jake's arms. Kelly's only impression was of a delicate straw hat perched precariously on flaming red hair, muddy knees, and green shoes.

"He's dead, Jake! He's dead." The lined face that peered up from beneath the tilted brim was streaked with tears and dirt. Amid a spate of fresh sobs, she whispered, "Horatio is dead."

"Shhh, don't cry so, you'll make yourself sick." Jake pushed back the ridiculous hat and dried the tears from the face so like his own.

Reeling from shock and confusion, Kelly's tender heart went out to the lovely, distraught woman. She could only watch, though, as Jake tenderly smoothed the fiery hair. With her attention riveted on the grieving woman, Kelly was vaguely aware of a very erect, very correct figure dressed in black and white, hovering in the background. Only the incongruous basket of gardening tools marred the perfection of his clothes and bearing.

"What happened, Mother?" Jake had stemmed the torrent that dampened his shirt.

"The damn cat ate him!"

Kelly gasped, completely bewildered, and helplessly turned to the man who stood one pace away.

"Monroe, Madame." He executed a perfect bow. "At your service. Horatio was Madame's prize orchid."

Incredulously, Kelly stared at him. His placid expression indicated that it wasn't unusual for Jake's mother to grieve for a flower that had been eaten by a cat.

"Mother, why did the cat eat Horatio?"

"The silly thing thought he was catnip." The quavering voice grew stronger. "I wish it had been arsenic. For two years I've given poor Horatio the most tender, loving care, and just when he had begun to thrive . . . Why, hello, my dear, you must be Kelly."

Kelly was totally diconcerted. "Why, yes . . . I . . . Yes."

With little warning, she was encircled by small, slender arms that were surprisingly strong. A floral fragrance filled her nostrils as her own arms slid instinctively about the tiny body. It would be difficult, indeed, not to respond to such exuberance. Obviously, whatever this vibrant, flame-haired woman might feel, she would be fierce and overwhelmingly intense.

"Now, let me look at you." She put Kelly from her gently and her wise eyes searched the young face. Then she gave one quick nod, apparently satisfied within her own mind on some point. "Yes, you're every bit as lovely as Jake said you were."

"Thank you, Mrs. Caldwell."

"No, no, no. Call me Lily, dear."

"Lily?" Confusion flickered across Kelly's face. It was there only fleetingly, but Lily's keen eyes missed nothing.

"I suppose Jake told you my name was Victoria." She sighed. "It is my legal name, but years ago my husband decided that I was like the lily of the valley, his return to happiness."

Mrs. Caldwell, or Lily, spoke as if she expected Kelly would understand exactly what she meant. Not for the world would Kelly admit she was bewildered. But again, she had not reckoned with the astute Lily.

"Don't you know the language of flowers, Kelly?" she asked gently.

"No, I'm afraid I don't."

"Ahh, then you don't know that each flower has a message and that each of us is best represented by a flower?" Lily studied Kelly intently, delving deeply into the secrets of the tawny eyes. "I think for now you're a yellow chrysanthemum. You'll always be a chrysanthemum, but I suspect your color will change soon."

It was a cryptic remark, but Kelly chose not to ask for an explanation. At least not for a while.

"Did you know Jake is almost a cedar?"

"Mother. I'm sure Kelly's fascinated by your flowers, but could you, perhaps, continue with her education at another time? She's very tired, and there's the baby to consider, you know."

"Good heavens! Forgive me, dear." She patted Kelly's cheek with a work-roughened hand. "What must you think of me? Of course you must be tired, and of course the baby will need all the care we can give him."

"Her," Jake supplied quietly.

"Ahh, you've already decided then, have you?"

"Yes. Our baby will be a girl who looks exactly like her mother." Jake's eyes lingered on Kelly's full-curving mouth. Something about the openness of his stance beckoned her to his arms. One step and she would be in his embrace. Could she? Should she? Kelly hesitated, unsure, and the magic was lost. The look in his eyes altered subtly and Jake turned away, leaving Kelly feeling oddly bereft. She fought to still her pounding heart, remembering that that look had not been meant for her. It had been a calculated part of his plan. It meant nothing. She *mustn't* forget!

"Then a girl it shall be." Lily accepted Jake's pronouncement as if it were fact, as if the baby would not dare to be a boy.

"Mother," Jake prompted gently.

"Oh, yes, Kelly must rest. Jake, you get her luggage, and Monroe will . . . Where is that man? It's always so irritating. He's never around when I need him." Lily turned around and ran full tilt into the waiting man.

"Monroe! Where on earth have you been?"

"Here, Madame."

"Oh. Well then, don't just stand there. Show Mrs. Jake to her room."

"Yes, Madame." He turned to Kelly, once more executing the perfect bow. "If you would, please, Mrs. Jake."

Kelly was left with little choice but to follow. It was phrased as a request, but she suspected that Monroe was accustomed to giving quiet, unobtrusive commands. She was tired anyway, and was longing for the comfort of a soft bed. Exhausted as she had been by the long day and late dinner, worry about this meeting had kept her from sleeping until dawn had streaked across the morning sky. She had said nothing to Jake, dreading to see the look of concern that sprang so often to his eyes.

She flashed one last quivering smile at Jake, then followed Monroe. She didn't know that the older man slowed his steps to accommodate her faltering ones, nor that by the weary slump of her shoulders, Jake could read her fatigue. Nor could she realize that he was cursing himself for so stupidly allowing her infectious enthusiasm the day before to lure him from the path of common sense.

Jake was learning, to his dismay, that where Kelly was concerned he could not say no. A chuckle rumbled in his chest as he remembered how captivating she had been in her innocent pleasure of the island and the sea. He watched until the heavy doors shut her from sight and only then turned his attention to their luggage. Lily stood at his side, watching her tall, proud son, smiling.

Though he walked with slow, measured steps, Monroe left Kelly little time to absorb the grandeur of the house. She managed only a quick glance of admiration for the twin staircases that met in the foyer, then twined upward in opposite directions to the separate wings. They were the famed flying stairs of southern plantations, as rare as they were beautiful. Even in her fatigue, she felt this was an enchanted house. As she mounted the stairs, she couldn't suppress her laugh as she remembered the last set of stairs she had climbed. Here there was carpeting rather than dirty, splintered wood, and delicate wallpaper rather than graffiti.

"Mrs. Jake, is something wrong?" Monroe paused on the landing, his voice bland, his expression neutral.

"I'm fine, thank you, Monroe." She graced him with a smile, its radiance banishing fleetingly the tension from her face. But nothing could hide her weariness.

"If Madame would like to rest, I could turn down her bed." It was again a subtle command, delivered carefully in the guise of a suggestion.

"Thank you, Monroe, I'd like that." Still smiling, Kelly followed the gentle tyrant.

Soft sounds of the surf woke her. Turning to her side, she wondered where she was. Though there were louvered doors, there were none of the pastels or the light, delicate rattan furniture of the beach house. This room was dark and richly bold, its earth tones complemented by vibrant shades of green and muted creams. A leather chair, its massive arms bound by rawhide, sat in the corner. An open book lay face down on the table by its side as if someone had just left it.

Kelly's hand strayed across the smooth coverlet of the huge, handsome bed. Jake's bed. Jake's room! And the sound that had awakened her was the drone of the shower in the adjoining bathroom.

As if on cue, the shower stopped. Accompanied by the low, off key whistling of a love song, were the sounds of a man moving purposely about. Then he was quiet. But Kelly could imagine the rasp of the razor against his heavy beard and the fragrance of his cologne. She almost could believe she was a wife.

"Ahh, you're awake. Did you rest well?"

Startled and fearful that Jake might somehow read her thoughts, she stretched and yawned, turning away from his gaze. She saw the open book. "Have you been reading?"

"Yes. Reading and watching you sleep. Did you know that you curl into a tiny little ball with your hand against your cheek?"

Disconcerted, Kelly flushed. His watching her in those unguarded moments implied an intimacy that brought a sweet surge of desire. She watched with wistful eyes as he crossed the room. He was dressed casually in tan slacks and a dark-brown sweater. His pale-beige shirt was open at the neck, revealing the darkly gold, furry tufts at his throat. His hair, darkened by water, was slicked back unmercifully. As he sat on the bed by her, she blurted out the first thing that came to mind.

"Why do you do that?"

"What, Kelly?" His finger traced the tender curve of her lips.

"Why do you slick your hair back when it's wet?" Her breath was warm against his cool skin. Their eyes met and held.

"If I didn't, it would be all curly." He traced the smooth, straight edge of her teeth, finding them far more interesting than any curls. "Not a very masculine thing, is it?"

"But it would be beautiful." Kelly's breath was coming in short, quick gasps.

"Beautiful?" He laughed, intent on the exploration of her sensual lower lip.

"Yes. Beautiful," she insisted stubbornly. "And don't say it wouldn't be masculine. Nothing could make you less . . . less . . ."

He chuckled softly as the color bloomed again in her cheeks. "Would it make you happy it I let it curl, sweetheart?"

"Yes. Yes, it would."

"Then why don't you fix it?"

"What?" Surprise shook her voice.

"Touch me, Kelly. Run your fingers through my hair. Touch me as I'm touching you." His words were a groan as his fingertips brushed the tip of her moist, pink tongue. "Please touch me, Kelly."

She needed no other invitation. Her hands left the coverlet and slid slowly, agonizingly, up his chest, lingering at the hollow of his throat. She could feel his heartbeat, so strong and rapid as if he'd been running. Did he want her? Embarrassed by her bold thought, she snatched her hand away.

"No, Kelly. Don't stop. Please." He caught her hand in his and held it to his heart.

With a new confidence, Kelly slipped both of her

hands into his thick, damp hair. Slowly, lovingly, she rumpled it into springy curls. Delighted with her creation, she laughed aloud, a sweet, musical sound. Jake grasped her shoulders, barely able to restrain his strong need to take her completely.

"Jake." His name was a plea, an unnamed wish, that made a mockery of his resolve.

"God help me, I need to kiss you." But strangely, he made no move toward her. It was Kelly, her fingers tangling in his hair, who drew him down. Tentative at first, she touched her lips to his. Again, and then again. His fingers dug painfully into her soft flesh as his mouth closed hungrily over hers. There was a fierceness in him that would have been frightening had it not found its match in her. All thought of time and place was lost as his tongue slipped urgently into the dark, sweet cavern of her mouth. She welcomed him, meeting caress with caress and thrust with thrust. When he was gentle, she reveled in his touch. When he demanded, she gave what he asked.

Kelly didn't know how it happened or when, but suddenly he was no longer bending over her. He was stretched full length on the bed, his arms cradling her body close to his. As his lips left hers to trail slowly over her face, his hand moved caressingly over her body. He cupped the ripe fullness of her breast, his thumb teasing the nipple. Her strangled gasp quickly brought them back to reality.

"Damn!" He rolled away from her, clenching his hands as he stared angrily at the ceiling. "Fool!"

There was nothing Kelly could say. Like an idiot, she had thrown herself at him for the second time. Jake was a normal, virile man. Naturally he would take what was so freely offered. In shame, she turned away, curling into a small, tight ball of living misery.

"Kelly, love, are you crying? Don't. Please don't cry, sweetheart. You're tearing me apart. I'm a fool and I know it, but I can't explain. I've broken my word not to bring our charade into the bedroom, and I'm sorry."

At her fresh wave of tears, he gathered her into

his arms. Sitting on the edge of the bed, he held her until the storm abated. He murmured soft, incoherent words that she could neither hear nor understand as he waited.

"It won't happen again, you have my promise," he reassured her as he dried the last of her tears. "Now, if I go away for a while, do you think you could join us for dinner, or would you rather have a tray here?"

"I'll come down."

"Good." With a finger under her chin, he raised her head to see her eyes. The pain there threatened to destroy him. "I do promise, Kelly. Never again."

Not waiting for her reply, Jake quietly left the room.

Six

She hadn't meant to, but Kelly drifted back into an exhausted sleep, then woke on her own hours later. Well rested, her natural logic and common sense returned. Realizing that tension was to be her companion for the next months, she decided that it would not be her master.

She prepared for the evening with care. Cold compresses for her eyes, a shower and shampoo, makeup lightly applied with a skillful hand, and she was ready to choose her dress. While she slept, her clothing had been unpacked and hung in the huge closet in her dressing room. She studied the clothes for a long while before making her choice.

"This one, I think." She held the dress before her as she glanced in the mirror. "I'll be the golden girl tonight. If Jake calls me Sunshine, then sunshine I'll be."

Music was drifting through the house, joined by the murmur of voices as she made her way down the stairs. In the bright light of the chandelier, the gold silk of her dress shimmered, rippling and clinging with each step. The empire line with the slightly gathered fullness above the waist hid her swollen abdomen. Her breasts, never large, had become fuller with pregnancy. The soft swells and the shadowed depths between were enticingly displayed by the square cut neckline. She was not aware that Jake had moved to the foot of the stairs until she heard his sharp, quick gasp.

With her hand resting lightly on the curved railing, Kelly paused. The man who waited below her was dressed as before, but now his hair was a halo of short, crisp curls. The lights that had turned her own hair to a shining blond, glinted through his, streaking it with dark, molten gold. He did not speak, but extended his hand to her as she slowly descended.

"You're beautiful." His soft murmur broke the magic of the moment as he led her down the last of the stairs.

Her performance was about to begin. The smile she gave him, as sweet as it was soft, as loving as it was glorious, was calculated to entrance the strongest of men.

"Thank you, darling." She spoke in a husky drawl. "It's all for you, you know."

His hand tightened over hers and his eyes glowed mysteriously at her endearment. He muttered something she couldn't catch as he dropped a kiss into her fragrant hair. The hand that touched her face trembled slightly, but lost in the wonder of him, Kelly scarcely noticed.

"You truly are sunshine in that dress. It's perfect for you."

"Have you forgotten?" Her laugh caressed him. "You chose it."

"And you were stubborn about it."

"Obviously not as stubborn as you, since I'm wearing it."

"Only because I bought it when you weren't looking."

"Along with the nightgowns, the caftan, the dinner dress, and the jewelry. Not to mention more baby clothes than three babies could wear. Shall I go on?"

A mischievous smile lit his eyes and lifted the corners of his mouth. The quick, teasing kiss he dropped on her lips warmed her, igniting the desire she believed had been banked so well. It could have been the kiss of promise a lover gives in anticipation of joys to come. Kelly stared at his hands as they rested lightly against her arm. They were long, lean, and strongly capable. How would it be to have them on her body, seeking all the secret places of sweet response? What would it be like to feel the smooth edge of his bluntly cut nails tracing delicious patterns over her bare skin; or the hardness of his calloused palm again capturing the fullness of her breast, its roughness rasping against the tender tip? What would she do if those hands should stroke her lovingly, bringing her to the brink of untamed desire? What then of her resolve?

Inexorably her eyes lifted. She met his puzzled gaze squarely.

"What is it, sweetheart?" He was concerned by her sudden ashen pallor. Kelly lowered her gaze to the carpet and shook her head, not trusting herself to speak.

"Jake, stop standing there in the hall like a lovesick boy and bring Kelly into the library." Lily's amused voice broke them apart.

Kelly's pallor was exchanged for the glow of a blush, but she clung to her role, refusing to falter from the path she had set for herself, for Jake's sake, and for those he loved. Gracefully, she slipped her hand through his arm, hugging it close to her breast. Her silvery laugh rang out as he covered her hand with his. His head bent over hers, her face lifted to his, and their eyes met and held, filled with the secrets of new lovers.

Arm in arm they entered the library. Lily, for once without her hat and gardening tools, watched them from her seat by the window, deeply pleased by what she saw. Any doubts she might have had of this strange arrangement were gone, burned away by the heat of the love Jake and Kelly shared. "I wonder if they know?" she murmured to herself.

"Good evening, Mother."

"Good evening, Jake. Kelly, you look lovely. Like a daffodil."

"I thought you said she was a chrysanthemum. A yellow one to be precise."

"And so she is," Lily answered seriously, refusing to be drawn by his banter. "But that doesn't mean she can't look like the other flowers as she changes her petals."

"Ahh, I see. Doesn't *she* change as her petals change?" He seated Kelly on a sofa.

"Kelly will always be a chrysanthemum, no matter what her outward appearance," Lily insisted.

"Then Kelly will never change?" He sat beside Kelly.

"I suspect she's already begun to change. Perhaps she's already become a beautiful red chrysanthemum."

"Mother, you're wonderful! You make every day an adventure." He turned to Kelly, his arm extended behind her on the back of the sofa, his fingers toying with the curls at the nape of her neck. "When Scott and I were small, all the boys were jealous. Our mother was always the prettiest and by far the most interesting."

Kelly smiled to hide the swift stabbing pain at the mention of Scott. He had hurt them all. Absently, she turned her cheek into Jake's hand, comforted by its warmth.

"Your mother's still the prettiest and most interesting," Lily declared with a hearty laugh. "Who else wears putter pants with dirty knees? And these?" She spread her hands out before her. "Have you ever seen hands that looked more like they belonged to a lumberjack?"

"Putter pants?" Kelly asked curiously.

"That's the name the boys gave to the awful pants I wear in the garden. When they were small, they thought all mothers had dirty knees and rough hands."

"And red hair," Jake added.

A soft purring sound interrupted them and Kelly turned as Lydia, in a motorized wheelchair which moved smoothly over tile and carpet, entered the room. Kelly was struck by the beauty of the frail woman, who looked to be little more than a child.

Jake walked over to greet Lydia. The hand he took in his was thin, the skin nearly transparent, the fingers long, graceful, and shapely. Her voice, when she answered Jake's query about her health, was low and cultured.

"Lydia," Jake said, "I'd like you to meet Kelly, my wife." His voice held the pride of a new husband and his look again spoke of promises. Kelly matched it with a brilliant smile and a silent, seductive message of her own. Jake lost the thread of conversation, forgetting to complete the introductions.

"Well, I can see the honeymoon is far from over." Lydia's laugh was as lovely as she was. She offered her hand to Kelly. "In case you haven't already guessed, I'm Lydia, your sister-in-law. If we wait for Jake, it might be tomorrow before we're properly introduced."

"Jake, will you please stop pacing?"

"I can't help it, these women make me nervous." His voice was low, but many pairs of eyes lifted over tops of magazines to watch him.

"They make *you* nervous! You've scared half of them to death. They think you're some sort of madman. Can't you please either sit down or go for a walk?"

"How can you be so calm? Most of the women here look as if they could have their babies any minute. My God! What would we do?"

"For heaven's sake, Jake." Kelly pulled him down into the chair he'd left not more than three minutes earlier. "We're in an obstetrician's office. It's the safest place for you to be. At least if something should happen, you wouldn't have to do anything."

He leaned back in his chair, crossed his legs, uncrossed them, and stood. He checked his watch. "Richard said ten-thirty. It's ten-thirty-three. What's keeping him?"

"He's a busy man. I don't mind waiting. What's three minutes between friends? Now, will you calm down?"

"Mrs. Caldwell?" Kelly turned toward the white-uniformed nurse. "If you would please follow me."

"It's about time," Jake growled as Kelly followed the nurse. He was hard on her heels as they entered the doctor's office.

The dark-haired man at the desk smiled when he saw them. "Jake! How are you? I haven't seen you in weeks. And this is your new, mysterious wife." He beamed benevolently at Kelly as he gestured for her to sit down.

"Not so new," Jake retorted. "We were married last December."

"Fast work." Richard grinned and winked, and if he was curious about his friend's secret marriage, he didn't show it.

"Faster than you think," Jake muttered. "She's seven months along and look at her!"

"I am looking, Jake, and she's gorgeous." He grinned again at the blush that rose in Kelly's face.

"That's not what I mean. Of course, she's gorgeous, but what about *her*?"

"What about her?" Richard asked as he lifted Kelly's wrist to take her pulse. "Have you had any problems?"

"Of course she has." Jake answered before Kelly could open her mouth. "Something's wrong. She's too small."

"Any fatigue?"

"She tires easily."

"Are you eating a balanced diet?" With a practiced hand, Richard checked her throat for swelling.

"She doesn't eat enough."

"Do you drink plenty of water?"

"She forgets unless one of us reminds her."

"Have you had any swelling?" He glanced appreciatively at her slender ankles.

"Last week her right foot wouldn't fit into her shoe."

"Any nausea, dizziness?"

"She felt faint this morning at breakfast."

"Is there any history of quadruplets in your family?"

"Oh, my God!"

"Good." Richard laughed. "I thought that might shut you up. Now, Kelly, I'd like to examine you, then we'll talk some more. Mrs. Hopkins will show you the way."

Richard turned as Jake rose to follow Kelly from the room. "Jake, you can't go."

"Why not?"

"Because the examining rooms are for patients only. No exceptions."

"But I'm worried about her."

"I can understand that. She's a lovely woman. Too bad she has such a terrible problem."

"What problem?" Jake's face went quite ashen.

"I think it's sad that anyone so beautiful can't talk."

"Can't talk? Are you crazy, Richard? Of course Kelly can talk."

"Then why don't you let her, my friend?" Richard left him standing there open mouthed and red faced.

"Oh, by the way." Richard's head reappeared around the partially open door. "I'll get one of the girls to bring you some coffee. And Jake, do try to calm down. You're the worst expectant father I've ever seen. Whatever happened to the tower of strength who never lost his cool?" His laughter drifted back to Jake as he walked down the hall.

By the time they returned, Jake had consumed three cups of the dark brew that masqueraded as coffee. "It's about time. What took so long?"

"It was a routine examination, Jake. It took no longer than usual." Richard guided Kelly to a chair. They had liked each other instantly, sharing a quiet amusement at Jake's distress.

"Well?" Jake growled as he turned to face Richard squarely.

"Well what?"

"What's wrong?"

"Absolutely nothing. Kelly's perfectly healthy and so is the baby. You might expect him to weigh around five and a half or six pounds."

"Her. Isn't that awfully small?"

"A bit, perhaps," Richard admitted, "but considering Kelly's small build, that might be an advantage. He should be here in a little over six weeks."

"Her."

Richard looked at Kelly. She shrugged, both smiled, neither commented. "Now, about the classes—"

"You haven't answered my question," Jake interrupted. "Why is Kelly so small?"

"It happens this way sometimes, Jake. True, it's not usual, but that doesn't mean anything's wrong. My guess would be that she has very little amniotic fluid. She should be careful not to sustain any blows to the abdomen, but that would be true in any case. Now," he began again, "about the classes. You haven't time to complete them, but it would help to attend as many as you can. Learn some of the exercises and the breathing techniques, then practice at home when you can. Whether or not you decide to have natural childbirth, they'll help in delivery. Take this pamphlet. It has the schedule and some other good exercises."

"Thank you, Dr. Matthews." Kelly stood to leave.

"Just Richard, please. After all, we can't have the wife of my best friend calling me doctor, can we?" He chuckled as he looked at Jake. "I've known this man all my life and I've never seen anything to compare with his behavior today. I wouldn't have thought any woman could throw him as badly as you have, Kelly. But it's nice to see. Not all of my patients are so crazy about each other."

"You talk too much, Richard." Jake grasped Kelly's arm and led her from the office.

Neither of them spoke about the visit or Jake's behavior until later that night as Kelly lay comfortably in bed watching him. In the few days she had been there, she had become surprisingly relaxed with him. There had been none of the painfully embarrassing moments she had expected in sharing his room. Jake scrupulously waited each evening until she was in bed and almost asleep before he joined her. Many nights they were quiet. But sometimes they would talk drowsily, with the wide expanse of the huge bed a barrier between them. Then, each morning when she woke, he would be gone.

"You didn't need to be rude," Kelly said. Her eyes were closed as she listened to the familiar sounds of Jake readying himself for bed. "Richard's a nice man and you were insulting."

"He's used to it," Jake said shortly, uncomfortable with the memory of the fool he had made of himself. It was a most unfamiliar feeling.

"I'm not."

Jake's head turned toward her in surprise. "I'm sorry, I didn't mean to embarrass you. It's just that I was so damn worried. I was afraid something dreadful was wrong, that something was going to happen to you and the baby."

"You loved him a great deal, didn't you?"

"What?" He was disconcerted by her rapid change of subject.

"You must have loved Scott a lot, or you wouldn't be so concerned about his child. Don't worry, Jake. I won't do anything foolish. I'll take care of his baby, then he won't really be gone. It's a part of him to cherish." Her voice trailed away as she fell asleep, and she missed the grim twist of Jake's lips.

It was long past the dinner hour when Jake let himself into the house. It had been a day of anger and frustration and memories. He had dealt today with the company whose contract Scott had nearly lost. This past week he had worked relentlessly to catch up on the neglected account. After the accident the board members had been considerate, waiting patiently during Jake's recovery, but now their patience had come to an end.

As he worked, Jake had tried to keep the memories at bay. But he could still hear Scott's frantic voice over the phone, asking for help. Jake had driven out to the company, smoothed the ruffled tempers, then watched in dismay as Scott slammed out of the office.

By the time he had reached the parking lot, Scott had driven away at a breakneck speed. The dreadful premonition that had gripped him then was a warning of what was to come. In a matter of minutes, he had watched helplessly as Scott's car crashed down the Georgia mountainside.

The memory had been a living thing, dark and painful. All he wanted now was to be with Kelly, to listen to her low, soothing voice, to watch her smile, and if he could find an excuse, to take her in his arms.

Tossing his jacket over the stair railing and loosening his tie, he walked to the library. Lydia and his mother were there, poring over a seed catalogue. Monroe was clearing away the last of after dinner coffee. Kelly was not there.

"Mother. Lydia." He nodded as he crossed to the bar.

"Jake! You look so tired."

"It was a bad day, Mother. Not one I'd like to repeat."

"Have you had your dinner?"

"I grabbed a sandwich at my desk." He downed his drink in one gulp. "If you'll excuse me, I think I'll go check on Kelly."

"But Jake," Lydia said, "Kelly's not here."

He was suddenly utterly still. Nothing moved but a muscle in his jaw. His hands clenched around the glass until Lily flinched in fear that it would break. "Where is she?"

"Surely you knew it was her first night for the Lamaze classes."

"I'd forgotten." Relief flooded through him, followed by self-reproach, then unreasoning anger. "Why didn't she remind me?"

"I think, dear," Lily said gently, "that she didn't want to bother you."

"Bother me!" He set the glass down on the table with a crash. "What in hell does that mean?"

"Simply that she was worried about you. You've been working far too hard since you got back, and she didn't want to add to your troubles."

"That's ridiculous! She's no bother, and since when did she take it on herself to make my decisions?"

"Jake," Lydia interposed, "she was only thinking of you."

"How did she go?" he growled, ignoring Lydia's explanation. "Who took her? Surely she isn't driving at night alone."

"I drove her," Monroe answered calmly. "I am to pick her up at ten o'clock, sir."

"That won't be necessary." Jake pulled his tie off and began unbuttoning his shirt as he walked from the room. "As soon as I change, I'll take care of her."

"Oh my," Lydia said into the quiet that followed the furor. "Poor Kelly. I've never seen Jake so angry."

"I shouldn't worry, dear." Lily's smile was that of a pleased Cheshire cat. "I think Kelly will be able to handle him quite nicely. Now, where's my other seed catalogue? Monroe? Monroe? Where is that man?"

"Here, Madame."

The sight that greeted Jake was a startling one. The gym floor was covered with brightly colored mats and a sea of bellies. Nine large, round, and firm bellies, and one that was flat. Each woman had a pillow under her head and one under her knees, and a man kneeling by her side. Kelly was alone.

"All right, class," the instructor said, "We'll practice shallow chest breathing."

Jake's heels clicked softly on the floor as he made his way to Kelly. He had changed into jeans and a crimson sweatshirt and his hair tumbled in a mass of curls that shone under the lights. Since pregnancy doesn't blind a woman, he was watched by nine pairs of appreciative eyes, and one pair that was wary.

"Hello, darling." He stood at Kelly's feet, looking down at her, "I'm sorry I'm late. Did you miss me?"

Her wariness increased. He spoke words of love, but only she could see the anger that sparked in his eyes. Before she could respond, he was on his knees at her head.

"I suppose you're Mr. Caldwell?" the instructor said.

"I am indeed." Jake's gaze seemed to devour Kelly.

"Welcome. Now then, if you're comfortable, we will begin." She addressed the group at large. "Mother, extend your abdomen. Extend, extend. It should be quite firm. Father, place your hand gently over her."

Jake leaned over Kelly, hesitant to do as instructed. Interminable seconds ticked by as he stared down at her. Then, almost in reverence, he placed his hand on the tight swell. His touch was light as a feather.

Kelly was exquisitely aware of him. She wished again, achingly, that he was in reality her husband and the father of her child.

"Now for the actual breathing. Mother, take a deep breath. Expand the lungs fully. Release the breath only a little, then replace it with small sips of air. This will be like a pant. Never breathe deeply, keep it short and shallow. Father, with your hand between her breasts, spread your fingers over her chest and down her sternum. Gauge the depth of each breath. Coach her, help her judge her rhythm. Keep the breathing shallow. All right. Hands on the abdomen? Hands at the breast? Then we will begin. Breathe."

Jake was hesitant again. He had shown little control before when he'd touched her. Could he do this and remain the calmly dispassionate person Kelly expected? It was too soon for more; she wasn't ready. Not while she carried Scott in her heart and his child in her body. He realized, wearily, that it was going to be a long, painful six weeks.

"Mr. Caldwell, you're not paying attention. Keep the rhythm, guide her. Remind her to extend those muscles."

Kelly concentrated fiercely on the words of the instructor as she pushed, extended, and breathed. This was a mental preparation for childbirth. The training of the mind to concentrate on the breathing rather than the pain. Perhaps it was a device she could employ now to block out the anguish of remembering that Jake touched her only because he must. It hurt. It hurt. Extend, breath . . . forget, forget.

A gentle touch, the warmth of long, lean fingers against her breast, and the soft cadence of his voice. This was Jake. Her strength, her courage, her friend, but never more than that. Extend, breath, breath . . . forget . . . forget . . . Would the hurt never stop?

For another half hour, the session continued. Surprisingly, Kelly did grow accustomed to his touch, and he with the coaching. In that time their troubles receded as thoughts turned to the mutual effort. They worked well together, almost as one, and for a time they did forget.

"That's it for this evening. Practice these at home, but be careful not to overdo. These exercises are to be used as late as possible in labor. Starting too soon would be tiring and at cross-purposes. But do practice and I'll see you here next week."

Jake rose in one fluid motion, offering his hand to Kelly. "Where's your sweater?"

"I didn't bring one." Her voice was as low as his. The other couples were laughing as they left, but Jake and Kelly didn't notice. They were painfully aware of only each other.

"Didn't it occur to you that it might be chilly when you finished?" His voice dropped to an even lower tone.

It was there again beneath the anger, the look with the impact of a touch. Desire was there, barely masked, its soft incandescence burning through her like a fever. Kelly closed her eyes, desperate to block him from her sight. Only then could she bring herself back to truth and reality. It was the anger, secret and inexplicable, that was for her. The desire, purposely only barely hidden, was for the benefit of others. He was a master at the game, she thought bitterly. With a look and a touch he could draw from her the response he wanted, insuring that she, too, played the game.

But it wasn't a game to her, she cried silently, and suddenly the bitterness gave way to uncontrollable anger. Damn him! How dare he do this to her?

"Chilly in Charleston, Jake?" she purred, her flashing anger nearly scorching him. "I have sense enough to know when I do or do not need a sweater. This"—she patted her stomach emphatically—"is the child. I'm a woman, and I'd appreciate it if you would treat me as such!"

She was magnificent! Her eyes were glittering with the topaz lights of tiger's eyes. The flush that flooded her cheeks heightened the smooth texture of her skin. Her mouth, trembling with the force of her rage, was richly passionate. The defiant tilt of her chin exposed the most kissable arch of her graceful throat.

There was no answering anger in him. Instead, he had to restrain himself from taking her flaming beauty into his arms, subduing the caldron of her wrath, seeking to turn it to a fierce desire that matched his own. He had no doubts that he could. He had seen the languorous looks that sometimes passed fleetingly over her face. She was a normal woman, one who had known love and desire. The love was lost, but the desire remained.

Jake didn't underestimate his skill with women. He had stoked the fires of feminine desire countless times. But desire wasn't enough from this woman. Never from Kelly, a jewel found, misused and cast away in a neighborhood bar, yet with its beauty and fire undimmed. He knew the passion that smoldered deeply within her. Dear God! What would it be like to be the man in her life when she loved again?

In an instant of unthinking madness, he almost reached for her then.

"Better take her home, Mr. Caldwell. What you're thinking is illegal, at least here it is." The cheeky comment was delivered by a grinning teenager, whose mixture of ancient wisdom and childish naiveté was too innocent to be annoying.

"Jimmy!" Jake strangled on the name as he turned from Kelly, his fist clenching and unclenching. "What are you doing here?"

"Candy and I got married this summer and we're expecting a baby now, same as you." The smile he gave the teenaged girl at his side whose middle bulged with the advanced stages of pregnancy, was radiant with adoration. The fact that the pregnancy had obviously preceded the marriage did nothing to dim his evident enthusiasm. The young falsetto voice dropped to a conspiratorial whisper. "It's great having someone special to love, isn't it, Mr. Caldwell?"

"Yes, Jimmy, you're right. It's great." With bleak eyes, Jake watched the young couple leave, happily engrossed in each other. He suddenly felt foolish and small minded for the jealousy that twisted through him. Thirty-two and a wealthy man of the world, he envied a callow boy with life's hard knocks before him.

He turned back to Kelly as something seemed to soften inside him. He took her arm gently with a slight shake of his head. "It's been a long day, Kelly. Let's go home."

Kelly had taken her shower and had settled herself in bed to read when Jake came into their room.

"Are you exhausted, Kelly?"

"Tired, but not exhausted."

"Do you feel up to talking?"

"If you like."

"I would. There are some things we need to settle between us."

"All right, Jake." She patted the bed. "Come sit by me."

She watched him as he crossed to her side. He was a handsome man. She had seen how the other women had watched him, and felt a strong surge of pride.

"Kelly"—the bed dipped beneath his weight as he

sat—"in Atlanta we decided that this would only work if we were totally honest with each other. That we had to keep the channels of communication open."

"I remember."

"Then what went wrong tonight? Why did you shut me out?"

"Shut you out!" Her eyes flew to his in complete astonishment. "Is that what you think I was doing?"

"Weren't you?"

"Of course not! You'd been working so hard and it was just a simple class, Jake. I didn't dream you'd want to go."

"Don't you think you should have given me the choice?"

"I'm sorry. It's not as if . . ."

"As if the baby were really mine? Is that what you mean, Kelly?"

She could only nod, struck silent by the pain in the depths of his eyes.

"But she is my baby, sweetheart, in every way that counts. I'll be the only father she'll ever know, and I'll love her and protect her for as long as I live. Everyone else believes that, Kelly, why can't you?"

"I'm so sorry, Jake," she mumbled.

"Sorry isn't good enough. You've got to forget that this is pretend. Tonight when I had my hand on your stomach, she moved. For the first time, I felt my daughter move! It was one of the most exciting experiences of my life. Then I was angry at you for shutting me out, for not sharing this time with me."

"She really is your child, isn't she?" Kelly breathed a glad sigh as her heart filled to overflowing.

"Isn't that what I just spent the last few minutes telling you? I wasn't there at her conception, but I'll be with her every other step of the way."

Happy tears began to spill down Kelly's cheeks. "Oh no! I don't want to do this," she half laughed.

"Do what, sweetheart?" Jake gathered her gently into his arms.

"I was going to stop being a silly, weepy woman."

Jake's laughter shook her as he hugged her close.

"You go ahead and cry all you want to. It's a pregnant woman's prerogative, remember?"

"Beast." She snuggled against him. "Stop laughing at me."

He stroked her face, brushing away her tears. "I wish you'd laugh with me, so I could see your dimples."

She giggled. "You have a fixation about dimples!" she accused.

"Only yours, love, only yours." He set her from him, kissing her forehead. "I'm tired. I think I'll turn in, too, if you don't mind."

Kelly lay listening to the shower, then to the sounds of Jake dressing for bed. She was contented as she had never been before. Something special had passed between them tonight, something she could hold in her heart.

"Kelly." Jake slipped between the sheets. He had dressed in dark brown pajamas and his hair curled damply about his head. "You look lonely. Come here."

It was an invitation she couldn't refuse. She slid quickly across the bed into his waiting embrace. With her head pillowed against his chest and his breath teasing her hair, she wondered how it was possible to feel such joy, even as she ached for a love that could never be.

For the first time, Kelly slept in Jake's arms.

Seven

Kelly stretched luxuriously, savoring the comfort that surrounded her. From the sheet that tickled the tip of her nose rose the aroma she had come to associate with Jake. He had been up and gone, probably for hours, but there was always this to remind her that he had been by her side. She touched his pillow that still held the imprint of his head, wondering how it could be that she had grown so relaxed. She no longer slept hovering at the edge of the bed, and often dreamed that she was safe and sheltered in his arms through the night.

In this euphoric state of mind, she dressed hurriedly, eager to begin the day. With the glow of good health sparkling in her eyes, she almost skipped down the stairs to the dining room.

"Good morning, Monroe. Where is everyone?"

"Madame and Mrs. Scott are in the greenhouse choosing the flowers for the table this evening. If Mrs. Jake would sit, I will fetch her breakfast."

"It's late, you have your other duties, I'll manage for myself," she said.

"It's no bother." He pulled a chair from the table, waiting patiently.

Sighing, understanding that she had again been outmaneuvered, Kelly sat, smiling as she watched his retreating back. Stiffly erect, he disappeared into the kitchen, then returned almost immediately with a tray filled with enough food for two.

"Thank you, Monroe, but I can't possibly begin to eat all this. When will you and Jake realize that eating for two doesn't mean eating twice as much?"

Realizing that he was imperturbably adamant she admitted defeat, and under his watchful eye managed a goodly portion of all but the toast.

"Good morning, Kelly." Lydia's chair moved so quietly that neither had heard it. "Monroe, Lily needs a special pair of shears. She said you'd know which she meant."

The slightest flicker of a frown crossed his face, then was gone. Torn between his duty to the two young women and his loyalty to his mistress, Monroe hesitated for a rare second.

"It's all right," Kelly assured him. "We can manage. Lily's probably waiting for the shears."

"Very well." He bowed and left, and Kelly and Lydia smothered the giggles they wouldn't dare let him hear.

"Poor Monroe," Lydia said when they were certain he would be searching in the garden shed for Lily's shears. "He has his hands full trying to care for three women, but he enjoys every minute of it."

"Do you think he realizes what a martinet he is?"

"No, he'd be appalled at the idea. The perfect butler would never dream of imposing his opinions on his employer." Lydia tried to keep a straight face, but failed miserably, succumbing to a fresh spate of giggles.

"Be sure that you put George in the corner and Herman over by the window. He sulks if he doesn't get enough light. I really would like for Roger to come tonight, but the smoke would bother him. Oh, hello, girls." Lily, dressed as usual in a flowing designer blouse, a floppy straw hat bound by a matching scarf, and a pair of violently green putter pants, stood at the door. Monroe hovered in the background, his face framed by the curling fronds of the giant fern he carried.

"Is there anything I can do to help with the preparations for tonight?" Kelly asked, hoping that Lily would say yes so she could keep busy and close her mind to her dread of meeting friends of the Caldwell family. When she woke this morning, wrapped in her feeling of well-being, she had forgotten the ordeal that was to come. Tonight would be her next test as an actress. Before a large audience, she must be a convincing lover and never for a second must Jake guess that every touch, every caress, and every word was true.

"What, dear?" Lily asked absently, then in the next breath said, "No, I don't need any help, but I believe Lydia had planned to ask you to help her do her hair. Hadn't you, Lydia?"

"I'd like that." Kelly turned to Lydia. "If you really want me to."

Lydia's smile was as shy as it was lovely. "I wouldn't want to overtire you before the party."

"Nonsense, she would be glad to do it," Lily insisted as she ran an appraising eye over Kelly. "A little girl talk would do you both good. Run along and enjoy yourselves. Now then. Monroe? Monroe? Where is that man?"

"Here, Madame."

With one last smile for mistress and servant, Kelly and Lydia crossed into the hall to Lydia's first-floor bedroom. Lydia led the way inside, then excused herself as she went to her dressing room to find the photograph of the hairstyle she had chosen for the evening. While she was away, Kelly had time to study the room, seeing the strong mark of the other woman's personality. Her attention was caught by two small, delicate watercolors hung by the bed. She was staring at them, entranced, when Lydia returned.

"They're beautiful, aren't they?" Lydia said.

"Yes. Whose work are they?"

"Scott's." The one word was filled with a raw pain that Lydia seldom displayed.

Kelly should have been ready for the answer. From all Jake had told her, she should have been prepared. But she was not. She swayed dizzily as the magnitude of what she had done to this lovely creature at her side spiraled through her, flaying her bruised sense of decency. The tears that she had only a few days ago sworn not to shed anymore, flooded her eyes. How could she go on? It was at least another month before the baby would be born, and after that, another six weeks before Jake would let her go.

She had no illusions. She knew he would be both worried and concerned about her. He would keep her here until he was sure she had recovered enough to leave, never realizing that each day she delayed would make it harder to leave him. If only she could leave now and not have to face the hurt in Lydia's eyes, nor ache with each lie she told Lily. If Jake hadn't found her at Nick's, she wouldn't be in this predicament. She would have managed on her own. Somehow.

"Kelly?" The gentle clasp of Lydia's hand drew her from her nightmarish thoughts. "I didn't mean to upset you. Most of the time I can control my bitterness. But sometimes when I look at the pictures and see the loveliness, then remember how Scott threw it away, I can't help but be bitter."

At Kelly's puzzled look, Lydia smiled. "Are you thinking that bitterness isn't the response you might expect from a relatively new widow? If you'd known Scott, you'd understand."

"Would you tell me about him, or would it be too painful?" Kelly's low voice was little more than a rasp as her throat threatened to close.

"It's painful, but probably not in the way you think." She nodded at a chair, then waited until Kelly was settled before she spoke again. "It didn't start with Scott's death, or even with his desertion. It began almost with the first moment we married. Jake has tried to protect me and he thinks he's succeeded, but I've known from the very beginning that Scott was never faithful and that he never loved me."

"Then why did you marry him?" Kelly burst out.

"Because I loved him and I hoped that someday he would learn to love me."

"Surely you're wrong. He must have loved you or he wouldn't have wanted to marry you."

"That's what I kept hoping, even as I knew all along that it wasn't true."

"Then why—"

"Why did he marry me?" Lydia asked kindly, not angry or embarrassed by Kelly's stammered question. "Because he thought Jake wanted me, for we were friends first. And as with everything in life, what Scott thought Jake had, he wanted. Poor Jake has spent his life stepping aside for Scott, only to watch him lose interest when the prize was his."

"And he thought you were the prize that time?"

"Yes. He wasn't consciously cruel. I don't think he ever understood what he was doing. He was like a child, always grabbing at the other's toys when his were better. He never forgave Jake for being big and strong, and an athlete. It was the one thing Jake *couldn't* give him, and the one time he couldn't step aside and by denying himself let Scott have what he wanted."

"And all the while Jake would have given anything to have a talent like this," Kelly murmured, looking again at the vibrantly lovely watercolors.

"It hurt Jake every time Scott destroyed some of his paintings. I only have these because he overlooked them. They were stacked among some unused canvases."

"Why do you keep them if they cause you pain?"

"They don't always. There are days when I can look at them and see only the beauty. Don't forget, Scott was never unkind to me, and for a long time he didn't know that his infidelity wasn't a secret. Jake still doesn't, he's tried so hard to keep it from me."

"Did you finally confront Scott?"

"We were arguing about it the day we had the accident that left me in this chair. He didn't cause the accident, but if he'd been watching the road instead of shouting at me, he might've been able to avoid the car that hit us." Lydia looked down at her useless legs and the silence stretched between them. "I'm sorry, I shouldn't have said that. The argument was my fault as much as it was his. Maybe more. I shouldn't have brought up the subject of his latest girlfriend while he was driving."

"Another of Jake's friends?"

"I'm afraid so. Jake can be so quiet and aloof. Scott could laugh and tease, sweeping a girl off her feet with a flair that could make her head spin. And foolish girls might mistake that for love." Lydia touched the controls at the arm of her chair and moved nearer to the pictures. With the tip of a finger, she traced Scott's signature. "I was finally going to leave him. I told him the day of the accident. But, in the end, he left me."

"He came back."

"No, not really." Lydia shook her head sorrowfully but firmly. "At least, not to me. He came back because he needed Jake. He was running from something again and he needed Jake's strength. No"—her voice sank to a low whisper—"he never truly came back to me."

There was nothing Kelly could say, nothing she could offer, except the secret protection from an even more painful truth. She cleared her throat as she stroked Lydia's hair.

"Why don't you show me that photograph? Let's see if we can copy it?"

Kelly dressed with utmost care. She chose a dress of emerald silk that enhanced her light golden tan. The fabric draped across her shoulders, meeting in a deep vee at the band that circled beneath her breasts. The skirt fell in soft gathers from the band to the floor. She looked pregnant . . . and quite beautiful. She was running a brush through her hair one last time when Jake tapped lightly and entered without a pause.

He stared at her without speaking for such a long time that Kelly began to fidget, feeling a flush stain her neck and face. She touched her cheek with fingers that were icy cold. "Do I look so terrible?" she asked.

"No, just the opposite. You're beautiful. It's only that I hadn't realized how much you'd changed in the past few weeks."

"I have grown." She looked ruefully down at her

bulging abdomen, patting it with her small hand. "It's the nature of my disease, but it isn't fatal."

He didn't laugh at her small joke; it was as if he hadn't heard. "I thought you were the loveliest thing I'd ever seen sitting on that piano bench in a smoke-filled bar, but I had no idea you could be this lovely."

"It's the dress."

"It's not the damn dress! It's you, Kelly. It's you, not your condition, not your clothes, nor anything else, and someday I'm going to make you believe me." He reached into his pocket and drew out a gold chain. As he wrapped it around his hand she could see an emerald stone in a delicate antique setting dangling from it. "You don't need this, you don't need any adornment, but I'd like you to wear it."

Quietly obedient, puzzled by his strange mood, Kelly turned her back to him. The chain circled her neck, the emerald falling between her breasts as his fingers fumbled with the catch. His breath was warm and sweet on her neck as he leaned near to see the tiny clasp. The effect was like wildfire in her blood. She wanted to bury her fingers in his sun streaked curls and draw his mouth to hers. She wanted to enfold him, make him a part of her, and never let him go. She was trembling with an awful need for him. He would see. He would know. She closed her eyes, willing herself back to some semblance of sanity.

"Kelly." His hands at her shoulders turned her gently to face him. She kept her eyes closed, not daring to let him read what she knew was there. "Kelly," he repeated softly as he brushed his lips across her forehead, "it's time. The others are waiting."

"I'm ready." She was appalled at the hoarseness of her voice, then profoundly grateful when he mistook it for fear.

"Don't be afraid, they're only people like us. Hold your head up and be the beautiful woman you are. There won't be a man in the room who wouldn't give his right arm to trade places with me. Now give me a smile, show the dimples." He waited until a small smile began at the corners of her mouth. "That's my girl. Remember, you're my wife and I love you. Now, let's go show them."

It was easier than she expected. From the time they reached the last step, they were surrounded by a bevy of smiling faces. It was obvious everyone there liked Jake, and that as his wife, she would be readily accepted.

Lily moved through the crowd laughing, chatting, playing the hostess to perfection. But she never forgot Kelly, catching her eye for an encouraging wink; bathing her in the warmth of a proud, pleased smile; giving her a touch, a grin, or a pleasant remark in passing; lending her support, from near or far.

Lydia, serenely regal in her chair, watched and nodded her own pleasure at Kelly's triumph before her attention was captured by her companion. The man, tall and distinguished, with streaks of gray in his hair, never strayed from her side.

Monroe, passing through the crowd with trays of drinks and food, detoured often to Kelly. Before he left to replenish each tray, he inquired gravely if there was anything Mrs. Jake required.

Jake never left her. He touched her constantly, drawing her to him as he talked with friends. As they warmed to her natural friendliness, he grew silent. Once, twice, his hand brushed lightly up her side, his fingertips lingering possessively, holding her even closer. His eyes smiled down at her as he let the conversation flow around him. Brushing his lips against her hair, he breathed deeply. She smelled of lilacs, lemons, and sunshine, a fragrance as unpretentious as she. Kelly laughed in delighted response to a comment Jake never heard. His smile deepened as he watched her animated reactions. She liked his friends, she was happy, perhaps she would stay. Kelly moved and, reluctantly, he let her go.

Kelly knew immediately that she would like these people. It shouldn't have surprised her. She should have known the Caldwells would attract people like themselves, people who were kind and warm. She leaned back again into the welcoming circle of Jake's arms, pleasantly aware of those who watched and smiled. A rather wizened but delightful old man made her blush with his blatant compliments.

"Jake, I hope you have the good sense to know what you have and hold on to her. She's an old-fashioned girl, I can tell. She'll be loyal and loving. A man can't have too much of that this day and age. You hold on to her, you hear me?"

"Thank you, Rufus. I know exactly what I have." Jake caressed her cheek, cupping her chin in his palm while his fingers stroked the high, sculptured cheekbone. Her eyes closed slowly. The brush of long lashes against his sensitive fingertips was the thunderclap following the lightning and a barely leashed fury pulsed through him. Hell! He had meant only to play the game, but how could he when she could do this to him with only an inadvertent touch and look? In clumsy haste he jerked his hand away, disgusted to find himself reeling from the impact of an innocent gesture gone awry. He didn't see the look of sad longing that crossed briefly, then was gone from Kelly's face. He only heard himself mutter, "I don't intend to lose her."

"There's just one thing." Rufus was warming to his subject. "You be mighty sure you don't wear her out having babies. It wouldn't be good for a little thing like her."

"Rufus!" Lily captured his arm in her hand. "Wouldn't you like to meet my new African violets, Julius and Hortense?"

"Julius and Hortense?" With a subtle wink over her shoulder, Lily led the old man away. Jake and Kelly were alone for the first time since the party had begun.

"Are you tired, Kelly?"

"No, your friends are easy to be with. I like them."

"They like you." He caught her hand in his. "Come on, I see two free chairs. Let's sit for a while. If we're very quiet, maybe they'll forget we're here and I can have you to myself for a minute."

"We could always hide behind George." Kelly tried

to keep a straight face, then burst into giggles at his questioning look.

"George?"

"The fern in the corner."

"Then George it shall be." He grinned as he snatched two chairs from their places against the wall and moved them into the corner, They were, indeed, somewhat hidden by the long, flowing fronds of the huge plant.

From their hideaway, they watched the guests as Jake entertained her with humorous anecdotes about them. His intention was for her to see them in a different light, as real people, not just the glamorous guests of the Caldwells. He wanted desperately for her to make them her friends and this her home. The electric tension that had shocked them both earlier disappeared as they laughed and talked in an easy fashion. The party surged around them and no one intruded into their private world. Jake's low chuckle blended with Kelly's musical laugh as they shared this secret rendezvous.

"So! This is where you've been hiding." A voice Kelly would never forget boomed in her ear. She turned to see Howard Norris standing at her elbow. "Did you two lovebirds have to steal away to have some time to yourselves?"

"Something like that, Howard," Jake drawled. But as with all gossips, Howard's skin was thick and he missed Jake's irritation.

"Surely you have her to yourself enough, Jake. After all, it's not as if you were newly married." Howard's voice dropped to a lower key as he eyed Kelly's protruding abdomen. "Or is it?"

"Howard!" Jake's chair banged against the wall as he stood abruptly. Several curious guests turned at the noise. Jake clenched his jaw and with a great effort mastered his anger.

"Jake, please." Kelly took his hand to help calm him.

"Never mind, Kelly." He patted her hand reassuringly. When he spoke to Howard, he met the avid eyes pleasantly, his anger not gone but tucked away safely. "Howard, would you like to see the dueling pistols I have in my study?"

"Dueling pistols?" Howard was disconcerted by the abrupt change of subject and disappointed in the failure of his ploy. "Uh, why yes, I would like to see them. Dueling pistols are a hobby of mine, you know."

"Good," Jake said curtly. He turned back to Kelly, bending solicitously over her. "Would you excuse us, darling? This shouldn't take too long. I'll be back as soon as this little matter is taken care of."

"Of course, my love." Kelly played her part in answer to Jake's. "Run along, but hurry back. I'll miss you."

"Only a moment, Sunshine, I promise." He kissed her quickly, then led Howard from the room.

Jake had hardly vacated his seat when a striking woman with thick, lustrous black hair slipped into it. "I've been waiting all evening for Jake to leave."

"I beg your pardon?"

"I wanted to talk to you alone, but it's been impossible. He hasn't left your side at all. We haven't met, by the way. I'm Marsha Gallagher."

"How do you do, Mrs. Gallagher? I'm—"

"Don't bother." The dark-haired woman waved a heavily beringed hand. "All of Charleston know who you are. In fact, they talk of little else."

"They do? But why?"

"My dear, you must understand. It isn't every day that the town's most eligible and elusive bachelor turns up with a mysterious wife. A mysterious, pregnant wife," she amended.

"Madame." Monroe stood over them, a tray in his hand. Negligently, Marsha lifted a regal hand toward the single glass. It was moved imperceptibly beyond her reach.

"Mrs. Jake will have the orange juice." He was stern, his eyes cold as he stared at Marsha with the proper vacancy of the perfect butler. He turned to

Kelly, bowing deeply, and the cold sternness left him. "Mrs. Jake."

"Thank you, Monroe." She sipped the juice as he waited by her, reluctant to leave. She smiled and tried to assure him that Marsha Gallagher was no threat. "This is quite all right, don't concern yourself."

"Are you certain, Mrs. Jake, that there's nothing else you require?"

"Nothing."

"As you wish."

"Well, well." Marsha leaned back into her chair as Monroe moved away. "You seem to have won over the family watchdog. Congratulations."

"Marsha," Lily called from the group she was trapped with, "if you must have a cigarette, would you please move? Roger doesn't like smoke."

"Who's Roger?" Marsha frowned at the cigarette between her fingers, then looked about her in confusion.

"The fern." Kelly offered with a grin, knowing full well that this was George.

"Ha! Stupid fern and a batty old woman!" She ignored Kelly's gasp, so intent was she on her targeted subject. "As I was saying, congratulations on fooling the family's trained pet. But then, if you could fool Jake, you could fool anyone."

"What does that mean?" Kelly was nearly speechless before this vitriolic attack. It was a cruel shock after the open friendliness of the other guests.

"It's obvious, isn't it? Getting oneself pregnant to trap a man is the oldest trick in the book. But even so, you must be pretty good to have suckered Jake with it."

"Marsha!" Jake glared down at the unsuspecting woman. A killing anger suffused him. "I don't remember inviting you."

"You didn't, darling. But I knew it was only because Oscar was out of town." She gave him a simpering smile that was meant to be intriguing. "Honestly, why you southern men think a wife should sit home just because her husband is away, is beyond me." All pretense was discarded as she looked at him in open invitation. "I knew you wouldn't mind if I came with Howard."

"But I do." The cold steel of his words pierced her air of self-satisfaction.

"I beg your pardon?" Marsha was shocked by the latent violence in his tone.

"I do mind that you came uninvited. I mind that you've said the things you have to my wife. I mind that she has to breathe the same air as you. I mind that as a gentleman, I can't thrash you within an inch of your life and stop that vicious tongue."

"Oh, Jake!"

"Howard, get Marsha's coat." Jake spoke to the man standing behind him, but his cold gaze never left Marsha's face. "She obviously doesn't know it, but she's leaving. And Howard, if she should ever call you again to escort her to our home, you'd be wise to remember she isn't welcome here."

Marsha put up a brave, haughty front. "I'll just say good-bye to Victoria. I'm sure she doesn't echo your sentiments, Jake." In quick strides, she crossed to where Lily waited, Monroe one pace behind. "It was a lovely party, Victoria." Lily ignored the regally offered hand.

"Marsha, if I'd known you were coming, I would have brought the Japanese rose from the green-house. You're so like it."

"What a lovely compliment." The dark-haired woman preened, confident again.

"The Japanese rose," Monroe said. "Your beauty is your only virtue."

In the silence that followed Monroe's interpretation, Marsha visibly wilted. She had never expected the gentle Victoria Caldwell to insult her, no matter how subtly.

"Let's go, Marsha." Howard grasped her arm tightly and led her away. "Even I know when I'm not wanted, you should do the same."

"But I only said what everyone else has been saying."

"Shut up and don't make a bigger fool of yourself than you have already."

"Everybody knows that—"

"I said, shut up! The everybody you keep talking about knows absolutely nothing. They were married last December. I know, I saw the marriage certificate in Jake's study just now." Their voices had been growing progressively fainter, but the attentive guests heard the last remark clearly.

Jake smiled down at the toe of his shoe, hoping no one would see his pleased expression. He regretted Kelly's ordeal, but his purpose had been served.

"You took Howard into your study to show him the marriage certificate, didn't you?" Kelly accused him in a happy voice.

"Guilty as charged."

"I wondered where it was."

"*Our* marriage certificate, Kelly. I've had it all along. It hangs next to the dueling pistols."

Kelly laughed. "You're a sly one, but thank you."

"For what?" he asked innocently. "For simply establishing the date of our wedding firmly in the minds of the town cat and chief gossip?"

"Yes, for that among other things."

"There are some things I'd like to thank you for, too, but we'll discuss them later." His grin sparkled with mischief. "Let's forget this for now. I'd like you to meet the man who's been Lydia's shadow all evening. Come." He took her hand, leading her smoothly through the crowd to the small group clustered about Lydia's chair. A note of pride throbbed in his voice as he introduced Kelly to the distinguished man whose hand rested lightly on Lydia's shoulder.

"Hello, Kelly." David MacHugh smiled down at her from his great height. He had midnight dark eyes that twinkled with some secret amusement. His hair shone like the blue-black of a raven's wing, with the gray at his temples a startling contrast. Kelly decided instantly that she liked him—not the least because of the glow that suffused his face each time he looked at Lydia.

He's in love with her! Kelly's heart lifted in gladness for her new friend. Perhaps this was the man who could erase all the hurts left by Scott's indiscretions. Maybe, if Lydia was receptive to him and with a little encouragement . . .

"I've been trying to get through the crowd all evening to introduce you two," Lydia said. "First you were mobbed, then you disappeared behind George, then Marsha gave her ridiculous performance. I'm sorry it happened, Kelly."

"So am I," Lily said, joining them. "I tried to head her off, but Sara Delaney had a death grip on my arm. I hoped my comment about Roger would at least shut her up until Jake could get there."

"Nice try, Mother, but Marsha couldn't care less about your plants."

"I suppose not." Lily grimaced. "But now I'm going to have to apologize to George. It makes him angry to be called the wrong name. Particularly when it's Roger's."

"Madame." Monroe cut short their laughter. "The buffet is ready."

"Good. If you'll sound the chimes, we'll go in."

"It's about time," Jake growled. "All Kelly's had since lunch was that damn glass of orange juice and she set it down behind George."

"I couldn't drink it. Marsha took away my appetite."

"Then maybe I can tempt you to eat more now." They started for the dining room, but Monroe forestalled them.

"Mrs. Jake?"

"Yes, Monroe?"

"I'm . . ." He hesitated, shocking all who listened, for no one had ever heard any but the most concise speech from this epitome of the gentleman's gentleman. "I am indeed sorry that I allowed that creature to approach you."

"Don't give it a second thought." Kelly patted his cheek affectionately. "You got Jake for me, that was enough."

"Thank you, Mrs. Jake." Color flamed in his face as he left abruptly.

"Kelly, love, I think you've made a conquest. Perhaps the most difficult of all," Jake drawled, and there was an odd light in his eyes. "Now, how about some food?" He offered his arm as he stared into her eyes. A sudden impatience for all the things he wanted and desperately needed was reflected deep in his own eyes.

"Am I too late for some of that food?" a man behind them said.

"Richard!" Kelly whirled from Jake to take the hand Richard offered. "I'm so glad you could come. I've missed you."

"I would've been here earlier, but the Sondhiem baby decided to enter this world slowly and reluctantly." At Kelly's instantly worried expression he chuckled. "Don't be alarmed, mother and baby are doing well. Lucy might be a bit tired, but she thinks Jeremy's worth it."

"Then you must be tired, too," Kelly said.

"Nope." His chuckle reassured her. "Bringing a baby into the world is more exhilarating than tiring." He gave Kelly a clinical look. "Tell me, does my favorite expectant mother feel as good as she looks?"

"Well, I don't know about that, but I do feel marvelous. Thanks to my most favorite and handsome obstetrician."

They laughed together, missing the dark look Jake shot them. The black, ugly shaft of jealousy that cut through him was a new and devastating thing. He resented the weakness violently and turned his anger on Kelly.

"If you two can tear yourselves away from your mutual admiration, perhaps you'd care to join the rest of us at dinner." He turned on his heel, leaving them to stare after him in astonishment.

Eight

"There, that's the last of them." Kelly straightened from her task of gathering the ashtrays that were scattered over, under, and across the furniture. Then spying one more, she knelt and reached far under the sofa, her head almost to the floor.

"What in hell are you doing?"

"Ouch!" Kelly banged her head as she jumped. She glared up at Jake who stood, hands on his hips, glaring back. "Did you have to creep up on me like that?"

"I didn't creep and you haven't answered my question. What were you doing?" He leaned over to help her rise.

"Leave me alone." Kelly jerked her arm away. "I'm perfectly able to get up by myself. I don't need you, Jake Caldwell."

"Perhaps you don't, but you still haven't answered my question."

"What question was that? I knocked it clean out of my head when you yelled at me."

"Dammit, Kelly, I didn't yell at you," he shouted. "And why on earth are you crawling around on the floor like a chipmunk after acorns?"

"I'm helping Monroe, if it's any of your business, and I'm not a chipmunk, acorns or no acorns."

"Monroe doesn't need your help. Get up." Again he moved to help her.

"I said leave me alone!" She folded her legs, letting her stomach rest against them, and crossed her arms over her chest.

"You're right," he said with a deceptive softness

that didn't fool her. "You don't look like a chipmunk. You look like a stubborn, little Buddha wearing a curly wig." He turned on his heel, leaving Kelly to sit open mouthed at the eloquence of his insult.

It would have been funny, if she hadn't been so angry. What Jake said was true, she did look like a Buddha. She should laugh, but right now she wanted to cry.

The night before had been beautiful. Even Marsha hadn't been able to take the glow from it. Kelly had been warmed by the loving protection of her new family as they closed ranks around her, showing the world she was one of their own. For a little while in the early evening she had forgotten that it was a temporary arrangement, and she basked in their love. Then, inexplicably, Jake had grown cold and morose, reminding her of their lie.

Richard, always kind and caring, had tried to cheer her. But all she could think of was Jake as he glowered at them.

After the guests had gone, she'd dawdled in their bedroom, hoping to speak with him, waiting long past her bedtime, but he never came. Finally, wearily, she slept. When she woke, the bed was rumpled, his pillow crushed, but Jake was gone. It was little comfort to her that he had been there; it was part of their deception. Yet, ironically, she had had the recurring dream that filled her nights. She had dreamed that he held her, murmuring softly to her in the dark.

This morning, in an effort to dispel her gloom, she'd insisted on helping Monroe. He had capitulated before her persistence, assigning her what he thought was an easy task, but he hadn't reckoned with an ashtray kicked under the sofa. Now Jake had yelled at her and she still hadn't reached the stupid thing.

Yes, she most definitely needed a good cry. She struggled heavily to her feet, deciding that more than anything she wanted to get away for a while. Away to think, to put things back into perspective, and to set her heart back on the path of truth.

She'd go to the beach house. She hadn't been there in over a week. She could walk on the shore and let the crisp sea air clear away the clawing despair that racked her. She thought of asking Lydia to accompany her, then dismissed the idea quickly. She needed to be alone.

Heedless of the new, ungainly bulk of her body, she raced up the stairs and changed into a heavy, red knit jogging suit. She scribbled a note that was hardly legible and hurried back downstairs. Tossing the small blue sheet of notepaper onto the table in the hall, she dashed out. The small swirl of air caused by the closing door blew the note from its place. It floated lazily like a paper airplane made by a child, then came to rest against a hall tree in the corner.

Almost furtively, Kelly walked to the garage and the car Jake had reluctantly given her to use. He objected strongly to her driving alone, and most especially driving to the island. As she backed the car from its space, it never crossed her mind that she was breaking her promise never to go there by herself.

It was a little before noon when Jake returned. He had been unable to concentrate on the mountain of work that cluttered his desk. He carried in his mind the sad but lovely picture of Kelly as she sat on the floor glaring at him, her lower lip trembling, her eyes shimmering with tears. Working had been impossible.

"Kelly," he called, eager to see her, needing to hold her and wipe away her sadness. He would apologize, then tease her until she smiled, and all would be well. "Kelly!"

Tossing his jacket aside, he strode down the hall to the library. It was deserted. A strange fear beginning to curl in his chest, Jake raced down the hall to the stairs, taking them two at a time. He flung their bedroom door open, not bothering to knock.

"Kelly?" His gaze fell on the slacks and blouse she had been wearing. They were thrown carelessly over the foot of the bed, something Kelly never did. He often teased her about her penchant for order. She would have to be very disturbed to leave her clothing strewn about. "Oh, God."

He hurried into her dressing room and grasped the ornate knob of her closet. He hesitated, fearful of what he would find, then opened the door slowly. He sagged in relief; her clothes were still there. Pausing only long enough to try to determine what she might be wearing, hoping it might be a clue to where she had gone, Jake clattered back down the stairs in search of his mother and Monroe. He found them in the greenhouse.

"Jake," Lily exclaimed, pleased to see him, but surprised by his disheveled appearance. "What on earth are you doing home at this hour?"

"Where's Kelly, Mother?"

"Why, I don't know. I suppose she's somewhere in the house."

"No, she's not. Monroe, have you seen her?"

"No, sir, not since early morning."

"Where's Lydia? Have they gone somewhere together?" He ran a hand distractedly through his hair.

"Lydia's having lunch with David today," Lily said.

"I'll call Richard, maybe—" He turned abruptly and left.

Lily smiled. Her intuition told her she needn't worry about Kelly and she was delighted to see Jake act, more and more each day, like a man in love. She turned back to her gardening as her eyes grew misty.

"Monroe?"

"Here, Madame."

"Ah, yes, hand me the pruning shears. Loretta has a limb that needs manicuring."

Jake stood at the water's edge, oblivious to his wet shoes. The island had been his last stop in a frantic search. Richard hadn't seen her and Kelly didn't like to shop. There was no place else. Straining his eyes, he looked up and down the beach. It was deserted. There was only the sound of the surf and the strident calling of the gulls to mock his anguish.

His heart thudded violently as he saw someone moving far in the distance. Afraid to let himself hope, he watched as a small figure in red trudged toward him. Sunlight gleamed on golden curls. It was Kelly!

"Thank God!" He ran the gamut from unbounded joy to raging fury as he raced across the sands.

"Jake." His name was a sigh on her lips as he stopped short before her. She stared at him longingly, hardly daring to believe it was he. Had she conjured him in her vivid imaginings, or was he real, towering over her so strangely silent? He flinched from her questioning hand, and then she saw his anger.

"Where in hell have you been?" His eyes were cold, piercing, and intense.

"Nowhere, only here." *In hell.*

"Nowhere," he mimicked. "Did it ever occur to you to tell anyone? Did you even think to consider that we might be worried?"

"I didn't mean to worry you." She spoke so softly he could barely hear her above the surf.

"You promised not to come here alone. Did that mean nothing to you?"

"I forgot, and I'm sorry." Kelly's shoulders slumped under the burden of weary tension.

"You forgot! Don't you realize you could have been hurt? You could have fallen here all alone." His voice grew ragged and unsteady. "You could have needed me and I didn't know where you were."

His relief unleashed an uncontrollable fury, a catharsis for his tormented mind, and Jake poured all his frustrations on Kelly's bowed head. She waited out the storm in numbing fatigue. There was no answering anger, no tears, only empty despair.

"I'm yelling at you, Kelly!"

"I can hear you." If possible, her voice had grown softer.

"Then, dammit! Don't just stand there. Tilt that stubborn chin and yell back!" Jake had been spoiling for a fight all day. The ugly jealousy of the night before had gnawed and torn at him, then been exacerbated by his worry for Kelly. He needed to lash out, to deny his hurt and fear.

"What good would it do?" she said. "I don't know what I've done or why you're so angry, but yelling won't help." She spoke hoarsely into the rising wind. "I'm tired, Jake."

Her calm, weary logic was like a painful blow to the stomach, cooling the beast that clawed him. As reason returned, he saw the ravages of her nearly sleepless night and this tumultuous day. She was exhausted, her face gaunt with sooty smudges beneath her eyes. He had done this to her. He and his black jealousy.

Then in total honesty, he admitted the raw fear that had brought him to the brink of madness. "I thought I had driven you away."

Kelly's disdainful gaze swept over her ungainly body before returning to lock steadily with his. "Where would I go, Jake?"

He had never in his life seen such desolation. There were no golden lights in her pain clouded eyes. No dimple marked her cheek. Where was the warm, vibrant woman who had entranced his friends? He had hurt her. Her pain became his and he thought he would die from it.

"How about here?" He opened his arms. "I'm not angry with you, sweetheart, only with myself. Let me hold you, please."

Kelly's soft cry was lost in the smooth fabric of his jacket as she accepted the shelter he offered. Chilled by the wind that whipped about them, she gave herself up to the comfort of his embrace.

"Can you forgive me, Kelly? I was trapped by my own stupidity. I've been a moody, stubborn, pig-headed fool." Kelly nodded into his shoulder and Jake chuckled. "What does that mean? That I'm pig-headed or that I'm forgiven?"

"Both." The muffled words drew a shout of laughter from Jake. He put her from him, but not far, framing her face with his hands.

"Friends?" He tilted her face toward his, pleased by the golden sparkle of amusement that had returned. With her consent, he swept her from her feet, holding her hard against him. "Then let's go home, sweetheart."

Giddy and elated by the resolving of their tension, content to be in his arms again, it didn't occur to Kelly to question the absurdity of his behavior.

Jake had no intention of explaining.

Days passed becoming weeks. Thanksgiving came and went with only a small family celebration to mark its passing. Kelly and Jake settled into a familiar routine. They played the loving couple until they were alone in their bedroom, and even there they had fallen into a teasing familiarity.

The Lamaze classes were attended faithfully and since it was almost Christmas, hardly a day passed that they didn't receive an invitation to this party or that. They attended several and Jake guarded her health zealously, never allowing her to grow overtired. Kelly was enjoying the placid contentment of late pregnancy when Jake dropped his bombshell.

"I beg your pardon?" She stared up at him from the bed. She had retired early to read and Jake had surprised her by joining her.

"I said, I think we should get married." His voice was low and raspy.

"You must be joking." In her astonishment she said the first thing that came to mind, then was sorry as she watched the dark, angry flush spread over his face.

"Marriage is hardly a joking matter, Kelly."

"I know, Jake. I'm sorry."

"Are you saying you won't?" His head drew back and the light dimmed in his eyes.

"No, no, of course not." She fumbled for the right words. "It's just that it's not necessary."

"I think it is."

"Why?" Her heart stopped, waited, hoped.

"As added protection for the baby. I want her to be my daughter legally, in case something should go wrong."

"I see." Something died within her. The sudden leap of improbable joy sputtered away. For a wild, foolish moment, she had dared to hope that he wanted her. She waved a listless hand. "If you're sure it's what you want, Jake, I'll do it."

"You needn't act like it's a death sentence," he growled like a wounded tiger.

"I'm sorry," she whispered.

"Quit that damned apologizing! Meekness doesn't suit you."

Kelly's head came up with a snap. "Damn you, Jake Caldwell! Hell will freeze over before I apologize again!"

"That's better." He grinned. "Now, can you be ready by the day after tomorrow?"

"I can be ready anytime you are."

"Good. I'll speak to David tonight. We could trust him even if he weren't in love with Lydia. As a judge, he can handle certain legal aspects for us." He started walking away and had almost reached the door when her courage failed her.

"Jake, are you sure you want to do this?"

"I'm sure," he said without turning.

"It will only complicate matters when it's time for me to go."

"You let me worry about that." The door closed behind him before she could say more.

On a bright, crisp December day, the day that should have been her anniversary, they were married. Jake made all the arrangements and a curiously unsurprised David handled the legal details circumspectly.

It was late afternoon when they arrived and were led into his chambers. His secretary remained to act as witness, and David assured them of her discretion.

At some point in the ceremony, Jake and Kelly

switched roles. She, who had been nervous to the point of collapse, grew serenely calm while Jake's supreme control deteriorated until his hands trembled and his voice was unsteady as he spoke his vows.

Under David's direction all went smoothly until the exchanging of the rings, and Jake discovered Kelly still wore Scott's gold band.

"Take it off," he rasped. "I don't care what you do with it, but you'll wear *my* ring now."

Nervously, she removed it, silently berating herself for forgetting. When her finger was bare, Jake slid the antique band he had chosen in its place. Kelly was startled when he lifted her hand to kiss her finger before he resumed his vows in a voice that was again calm.

"Congratulations, Mrs. Caldwell," David said with a broad smile.

"Thank you, David. You've been more than kind."

"No," he answered gravely. "You're the one who's been kind. I can never thank you enough for what you're doing for Lydia. Her marriage was a bad one, but this knowledge would have destroyed her. Jake's a lucky man, Kelly."

"I know that." Jake's long arm snaked around her, drawing her against his hard chest. Absently his fingers stroked her stomach, then he chuckled. "I think our little girl must be ticklish. She just kicked me."

David asked the inevitable question. "Jake, have you ever considered that this baby might be a boy?"

"Never," he declared as he kissed Kelly's hair. "A girl who's a carbon copy of her mother, that's what I'm expecting."

"Maybe we should have quadruplets like Richard suggested. Then we could have two of each," Kelly teased, relaxing against him.

"No way, Mrs. Caldwell. I'd rather have them one at a time. It's more fun that way." The look he gave her destroyed her composure as she thought of the joy of having Jake's babies. She shivered and put the impossible aside.

"We'd better be going." Her voice didn't sound like her own. "If we're late for our anniversary dinner, your mother and Monroe might become suspicious."

"Right," he agreed. "David, we'll see you Saturday for dinner when we put up the tree?"

"Lydia said seven o'clock."

"Good. Now, I'm going to take my wife away and buy her a wedding gift."

Kelly hadn't dreamed that really being married to Jake would change things, but it did. She felt as if the burden of her lie was lifted from her. Even Jake seemed to change. He relaxed, all the guards came down. Their friendship deepened and grew, as did Kelly.

"Oh, dear."

"Something wrong, love?" Jake was standing before the mirror tying his tie. They no longer avoided each other in the bedroom and could converse quite casually as they dressed.

"I can't reach this zipper."

"Then allow me." The quick rasp of the zipper was punctuated by the kiss he brushed on the nape of her neck. "All done?"

"Yes. I can hardly wait until we start decorating the tree."

"Promise me you won't overtire yourself tonight." Her enthusiasm was infectious and though he tried not to hover, Jake worried. "You will be careful, won't you. The stretching and straining can't be good for you."

"For heaven's sake! I'm not some delicate little thistle that a puff of wind would break in half, you know." She looked down at her considerable girth. "In fact, I think I look quite substantial. Rather like a bowling ball."

"You're the prettiest bowling ball I've ever seen." Jake laughed as he led her from the room.

The tree, a prickly evergreen, brushed the ceiling. Jake and David, with Monroe's help, strung row after row of lights. Kelly and Lydia had been given the unenviable task of sorting the ornaments, which the men then hung. Lily crawled on all fours to check that the burlap bag binding the precious roots was moist.

Restless with her inactivity, Kelly wandered closer to the tree. One ill-placed ornament had disturbed her all evening. She stepped up onto the footstool and stretched to move the pretty gilt angel from behind the snowflake. Her fingertips could barely touch it. She shifted and stretched again, teetering precariously against the tree.

"Dammit, Kelly!" She was snatched off her perch by Jake's large hands. He set her gently on her feet, glowering in exasperation. "Are you trying to break your neck or just bring the tree down on you? Good Lord, woman! Do you intend to drive me out of my mind before this baby gets here?"

"I was only moving an ornament," she protested.

"If you want an ornament moved, tell me, I'll move it. I'll move one, a dozen, hell I'll move the whole tree! Just don't get back on that stool." He paused in his tirade for a breath and a small smile curved his mouth. "Please?"

The smile and the last word did it. When he looked at her like that and spoke so softly, she could deny him nothing. She only nodded and smiled.

"No more stools?"

"No more stools."

"Promise?" he persisted doggedly.

"I promise."

"Then if you and Lydia have finished with the sorting, why don't the two of you play for us?"

"What would you like to hear?" Lydia's chair scraped softly against the floor as she drew it up to the piano. Her slender fingers began to move over the keyboard in random chords. It wasn't a song, but it became a haunting melody.

"How about Jake's favorite," Lily suggested.

Lydia nodded and began playing "Silent Night." Kelly joined her and soon the two of them were playing song after song. Some were low sweet ballads, others rousing folk songs. It didn't take Kelly long to realize that Lydia far outclassed her.

"I didn't realize you played," Kelly murmured as they began a slow and quiet duet.

"I don't much anymore."

"But why? Surely there's a demand for talent like yours. Where did you study?"

"Juilliard, for a while."

"You didn't finish your studies?"

"No, not quite."

"Why?"

"Scott." A single discordant note, heard only by Kelly's trained ear, broke the rippling harmony as Lydia's hands moved gracefully over the keys. "I was home for a break when I met him. He swept me off my feet and suddenly he was the most important thing in my life. I didn't return when the session resumed. I stayed here to be near him."

"Have you ever considered going back?"

"No, I'm not sure I'd want to."

"Is it the chair?" Kelly asked gently.

"Partly, but I'm not sure I'd want the life of a performer in any case. If I had, I don't think Scott could have swayed me so easily. I love music, but in my case it's useless."

"You wouldn't have to be a performer to put your music to use, Lydia."

"Then how else would I use it except for my own personal enjoyment?"

"Have you ever considered teaching? I don't mean a large number of students. There's always the talented young child or teenager who needs special attention. Wouldn't it give you a sense of accomplishment to help a young, budding talent develop?"

"I'd never thought of it, but yes, I think it might. I'll give it some serious consideration. Thank you, Kelly."

"It was nothing. But remember, if you need me, I'll help you any way I can. Now, why don't I leave the piano to you? I'd like to hear some of the wonderful music I know you can play." Kelly moved away to her seat, settling back as Lydia swept them away into a world of beautiful sound.

"Tired, sweetheart?" Jake whispered in her ear. His hand enveloped hers in a warm grasp. "The tree's done. Would you like to go up to bed?"

"Not yet, I'd like to listen a bit longer."

"Not for long. Christmas in Charleston can be exhausting. You'll need your rest for the festivities tomorrow. We all will."

"This is too nice to leave. Not just yet."

Jake smiled. With a soft look in his eyes he said, "I know."

As the fire burned low, its pale light bathing the room in a golden luster and with soft music swirling about them, Kelly was content. Before the glitter of an old-fashioned tree and with Jake by her side, she understood the magic of Christmas. In her world this night, there was peace and good will.

The child beneath her heart moved and she smiled, vowing to love Jake's daughter as she herself had never been loved. Kelly closed her eyes and, with her hand resting lightly on the swell of the child, dreamed of babies and Jake.

"Come on, sleepyhead. You'd be more comfortable in bed," Jake teased softly.

"I wasn't sleeping, only resting my eyes," Kelly protested.

"We've worked you too hard tonight and you weren't only resting your eyes."

"Ah, yes, slave driver." She smiled at him as she took the hand he offered. Of late, chairs had become her mortal foes. She could neither get into nor out of them with any semblance of grace.

"Good night, everyone," Jake said. "Kelly's been napping in her chair, we we're going to turn in now. Merry Christmas."

"Merry Christmas!" Lily, Lydia, Monroe, and David chorused.

Kelly hesitated at the stairs. The stairs frightened her. Now that she couldn't see her feet she feared a misstep or, worse, that she might topple backward. Her grip on Jake's arm tightened.

"Do the stairs frighten you?" he asked. "Don't lie, Kelly."

"I wouldn't dream of it." She wrinkled her nose at him, then gasped as he swept her into his arms. "Jake, put me down."

"I will as soon as I get you up these stairs."

"Idiot." She locked her arms about him and began to nuzzle his neck.

"Kelly." His arms tightened about her as he took the stairs carefully.

"Ummm?" Intent on her exploration, she didn't realize they were in their room until he set her down on the bed.

"You feel like playing with fire tonight, don't you, sweet?"

"Why, whatever do you mean, Jason Caldwell?" Kelly batted her eyes at him outrageously.

"I mean, little girl, that if I didn't know Monroe wouldn't let you near it, I'd swear you'd been drinking Grandma McDonald's special elixir."

"Me, sir? Never!"

"Don't flirt with me and think you're safe because you're a butterball, sweetheart. I could make love to you this very minute. Is that what you want, Kelly?"

She sobered instantly. Giddy from his nearness, she had almost given herself away. Color stained her cheeks and she refused to meet his eyes.

He grinned. "That's what I thought. Don't worry, sweetheart. I was only teasing. Now, how would you like to open one of your gifts? There's no law that says you have to wait until Christmas morning."

Kelly watched as he opened a drawer and took out a small package wrapped in silver and blue paper. "It's not much but . . ."

She caught the pretty package as he tossed it into her lap. He was trying to be nonchalant about it, but Kelly had learned to recognize the signs of tension. This was important to him.

She tore impatiently at the paper and the bow,

then more gently unfolded the tissue paper inside. When she discovered what was hidden in it, her dancing eyes smiled up into his, wiping away his fears.

"My first seashell!"

"Do you like it, sweetheart?"

"You knew I would." With shaking hands, she carefully lifted the clear paperweight from its box. A battered shell floated inside the graceful globe. "I thought I'd lost it. I looked through the others over and over again, but I couldn't find it."

"You gave it to me, don't you remember?"

"And you kept it . . . Jake!" She opened her arms eagerly, wanting to hold him.

As he leaned down for her hug, his own arms went about her. She was innocence and trust. It was little wonder Scott had been able to dupe her. Jake's breath caught harshly in his throat at the memory of his brother. Slowly, gently, he released her, drawing away from her embrace. In his own hurt, he didn't see the shadow that darkened Kelly's face, then was firmly hidden behind her bright smile.

"I talked to Richard today," he said, making a production of picking up the paper and ribbon she had tossed aside, afraid she would read too much in his face. "He's going to see you the day after tomorrow at two."

"Whatever for? Surely you aren't interrupting his holiday."

"No, he has office hours that day."

"But I don't need to see him yet. I'm not due to go back for another week."

"I want you to see him before then."

"There's no earthly reason for us to take up Richard's valuable time when I have an appointment a few days later."

"Humor me, will you? I have a business trip the day after, and I want to be sure everything's as it should be before I leave."

"How long will you be gone?"

"Three days, at least." He crushed the paper in

his hand. "Damn! It couldn't have come at a worse time. I don't want to leave you."

"The baby's not due for two more weeks. I don't think anything will happen while you're away, but I'll see Richard before you go if it'll please you." She capitulated before his anxious concern.

"Thank you, Kelly. I'll feel better if I'm sure there's no danger of the baby coming when I'm away."

To the left, inhale, exhale. Inhale, exhale. To the right, inhale, exhale. Inhale, exhale. Kelly sat on a mat spread on the floor. Her legs were crossed at the calves, her back straight, one hand on her knee, the other on the floor. Then she shifted. Each time she did the exercise, she could feel the ache in her back ease. Since Jake had been away, she had exercised alone and she missed his foolishness terribly.

Poor Jake. He had gone from worry over her lack of size, straight into a tailspin when she had bloomed overnight. Richard had been hard pressed to make him believe that her pregnancy was progressing quite normally.

"How in the hell do you expect me to believe that for her to suddenly . . ." He had searched for the right word and apparently couldn't find it. "Look at her, Richard! She's as round as she is tall! Something's wrong. Nothing changes that fast."

"Kelly did," Richard said calmly.

"Yes, she did. Now tell me why."

"Jake, there's nothing to tell. It happens this way sometimes. As long as everything keeps going as it is, there should be no problem."

"Should! What do you mean *should*? Don't you know? You're the doctor, you're supposed to know."

"Jake, if I didn't know you so well and if I didn't love you like a brother, I think I'd punch you in the nose." Richard strained to keep his patience. "Now, take your beautiful wife home. She's tired, I'm tired, and after this tantrum you should be tired."

From that visit, Jake seemed to calm down, taking her astonishing figure in stride. He still hovered, sometimes to the point that she wanted to scream, but at least he wasn't so frantic.

Kelly shifted positions, this time to her side for the leg lifts. "Lift, inhale. Lift, exhale. Down, down. Lift, inhale. Lift, exhale. Down, down."

The exercises that had been so much fun with Jake were dreadfully boring now. She missed the sly comments he made as he kept count for her. He had a singsong routine that kept her going and laughing. Kelly could almost hear him now.

"Breathe, Buttercup, breathe. Lift, lift, breathe."

"You just call me that because it's as close as you dare to come to Butterball," she accused.

"You said that, I didn't. Breathe, Buttercup, breathe. Inhale, exhale, tighten, tilt. Say, kiddo, do you remember when I used to think you should be bigger? I wished you would look like the other women in Richard's office. I got my wish. Boy did I ever! I just didn't expect Mt. McKinley."

"You only say *that* when I'm flat on my back."

"When you're flat on your back is the only time you look like Mt. McKinley. The rest of the time you look like a bag lady that has her belongings stashed under her dress. Breathe, Buttercup, breathe."

He'd been gone for two days. Kelly hadn't wanted him to go, but she didn't dare let him know. He would have cancelled his meetings without a thought. So, she had hidden her trepidation and worn a cheerful face. She had had lots of practice lately in fooling Jake. She still played her role of the loving wife for the world and they believed her. And in the bedroom she played the actress, even asking Jake if this little touch or that impulsive kiss had been right . . . and he believed her.

If only he weren't so kind, if he would be less generous and less concerned, then perhaps she wouldn't love him. Perhaps if his strange moods of tension and irritation came more often, she could curb this growing, living desire that was with her both day and night.

"Desire?" Kelly chuckled aloud as she sat up and

looked ruefully at what had once been her waistline. At a quick tap at the door, she looked up. "Come in."

"Madame is thirsty." Monroe stood at the door, a tray with a tall glass of water and a linen napkin in his hand. "The hour of exercise is over. If Mrs. Jake would like to rest, I will turn down her bed."

Kelly had grown accustomed to Monroe's gentle commands. Any suggestion that he hovered would be met with silent disdain. He was the perfect butler who did his job, but never intruded on family matters, or so he thought. Monroe was as much a part of the family as Lily herself.

"Madame." Monroe offered his hand, helping Kelly to rise as gracefully as one could with her encumbrance.

"Oh!" Kelly gasped in surprise.

"Is something wrong?"

"I'm not sure, Monroe, but would you call Dr. Matthews, please."

"Madame, are you in pain?" The hands that he clenched in front of him tightened perceptibly.

"No, no, don't concern yourself. It's just a little something I need to ask about." She flashed him a smile that deepened her dimples. "But I think I will lie down until I speak to Richard."

Nine

The double doors flew open with a crash, shattering the silence of the corridor, mocking the signs that constantly asked for quiet. The man who strode through them, his tie loose beneath an open collar and his hair in wild disarray, had little use for rules or signs. He strode purposefully, his heels striking firmly as each hurried step brought him closer to his heart's concern.

"Jake!" Lily rose from her seat in the tiny waiting room when she saw her son.

"Mother! Where is she? Is she all right? What happened?" He ran a hand through his hair, obviously not for the first time. "Oh, God! Why did I leave her?"

"She's in good hands, there's no cause to worry." Lily took his arm to lead him out of the flow of the hospital traffic. "Come sit here. We should be hearing something in a bit. Monroe and Lydia have gone down for a cup of coffee, would you like some?"

"No," he answered curtly as his eyes scanned the various closed doors, reading what was written on each. "Where is she?"

"In the delivery room. She's been in—"

Jake wheeled about. He had heard all he needed.

A small, quick witted young nurse darted from behind her desk to place herself between Jake and the doors that led to the delivery rooms. With practiced skill, she told him in a no-nonsense voice, "I'm sorry, fathers are not allowed."

"Move, lady."

"You can't go in."

"Watch me!"

His hands closed about her waist and he lifted her off her feet. Very gently he set her out of his way, then pushed through the swinging door. The first person he saw was Richard.

"Richard! Where is she? How is she?"

"I'm sorry, Doctor." The small nurse tried to wedge herself between them. "He just barged in."

"Never mind, nurse. I'll handle him." Richard took Jake's arm and led him into the doctors' lounge. "Sit down, Jake. Coffee?"

"No."

"No, what?" Richard laughed, enjoying his friend's discomfort as he poured himself a cup of the bitter brew. "No, you won't sit down or no, you don't want any coffee?"

"No, period." Jake was running on raw nerves and patience was a thing long in the past. "Dammit, Richard, tell me about Kelly. Tell me she's all right!"

"Sit down and stop acting like an idiot and I will."

It was a command and Jake recognized it as such. He settled himself into a worn leather chair by a low table, glaring at Richard in frustration.

"Good, now if you're calm enough to understand, I'll explain." With one leg hitched over the corner, Richard half sat on the coffee table, sipping from his cup.

"Blast it, man! Get on with it or I'll find her myself, if I have to tear every door in the place off its hinges."

"First of all, Jake, Kelly's perfectly fine," Richard said calmly, ignoring the outburst. "This morning after her exercises she noticed something not quite as it should be and very wisely called me. From what she told me over the telephone, I suspected what the problem was and after I examined her I was sure. She was losing amniotic fluids. Not a dangerous thing in itself, but it indicates a tear or an opening in the amniotic sac. This, of course, could lead to the introduction of bacteria and an infection. We were lucky she was so near to delivery, so we quite simply brought her here and induced labor. There were no other complications and she's as good and beautiful as ever."

"Why didn't you tell me about this the day before yesterday?"

"Because I didn't know about it."

"Why not?" Jake growled. "It's your job. It's what I'm paying you for."

"I'm a doctor, Jake, not God. And do you really think it's the money that matters at a time like this?"

Jake had the good grace to be ashamed at the last remark. "No, I don't, Richard. Forgive me. It's just that . . . Are you certain she's in no danger?"

"I'm absolutely sure. Why don't you come with me and you can see for yourself."

"Now? She's awake?"

"Of course she is. She was awake the whole time." Richard chuckled. "And in case you're interested, you have a daughter who's gorgeous, all five pounds six ounces of her."

"A daughter?"

"Yes, a daughter. Had you forgotten that the little protuberance Kelly's been hauling about would sooner or later be either a son or a daughter?"

"A daughter," Jake marveled. "Does she look like her mother?"

"If you'll come with me, you can decide that for yourself too."

"Kelly." Jake stood awkwardly at the door. Richard had shown him down the hall, then deserted him. Strangely, after these weeks of living so closely with her, he could think of nothing to say. All he could do was gawk, thinking how tiny and *flat* she was, and how very lovely. He tried again and this time his husky voice was stronger. "Kelly?"

"Jake." Her eyes were softly glowing as she looked at him and smiled. "You came."

"As fast as I could." He crossed to her side, surprised at how calm and rested she looked. "Were you asleep. Your eyes were closed."

"No, as a matter of fact, I was thinking about you."

"Me?"

"Ummm." She nodded. "I was wondering if you'd come today or if you'd wait until you finished your business."

"Wait! Are you crazy? Of course I came. Ask the highway patrol! I think I broke every speed record known to man. I came so fast"—he looked ruefully down at his empty hands—"I forgot to bring you flowers."

"I don't want flowers, Jake." Her voice quavered and her shining eyes swept over him as she murmured softly, "Just you."

Easy Jake, he warned himself, *she doesn't know what she's saying. Today's a special day and what you're seeing in her eyes is the overflow. She's happy and all the world's beautiful, even you.*

He wanted to take her into his arms, but settled for holding her hand. His long fingers laced through hers as he smoothed a feather soft kiss on the tender flesh inside her wrist. He couldn't see how Kelly's other hand hovered over his bent head, longing to touch his curls. When he straightened, reluctantly releasing her, her face was as calm and tranquil as his.

"Have you seen her yet?" she asked.

"No, I wanted to see you first. Richard said he'd be back in a few minutes. I'll see her then."

"I think you're in for a surprise." She laughed. "I wish I could be there the first time you see her."

"Why, does she have three ears?" he teased, loving the sound of her laugh, loving her, wanting her.

"No, just the usual number. But she's beautiful. Just wait, you'll see."

"Pretty proud of yourself, aren't you?"

"Yes. I'm proud of both of us. She wouldn't have been such a special baby if it hadn't been for you." At the soft sibilant sound of the tortured breath he drew, she faltered. Her heart lurched and she stammered on, babbling senseless inanities. "I mean, everyone knows that it's the happiest women who have the prettiest babies."

"Kelly." His taut voice cut across her heart-stricken blundering. "Never mind, I understand."

"No! No, you don't! I didn't mean to hurt you. It's just that I've been so happy, I'd forgotten what it might be like for you. She's going to remind you of Scott and his loss, and it must bring back the sadness all over again."

"Sweetheart, look at me." She refused. He tugged gently at a curl and she reluctantly lifted her gaze to his. "I'm not hurt and there are no sad memories to spoil this day. You're safe and healthy and we have our daughter, so what do I have to be sad about? Now, smile for me. You know what I want to see."

He watched as the lost, forlorn look slowly left her face. The first faint quiver of a smile lifted the corner of her mouth, trembled for an instant, then deepened into a happy grin.

"Aha! Dimples!"

The giggle he had been waiting for bubbled forth. The light that turned her eyes to amber sparkled back at him as the giggles became full-blown laughter.

"Jake." She grasped both his hands in hers, still laughing. "You're wonderful."

"I know." He tweaked another curl and laughed with her.

"If this is the mutual admiration society, I have another member for you." Richard stood in the open door, a pink blanketed bundle in his arms. "Since this is a special circumstance, I decided it called for special rules. Jake, may I present your daughter?"

Jake was utterly still. He sat poised by Kelly's side as if afraid to look. Kelly saw again the ragged shadow of pain cross his face, then disappear.

"Here, slip this over your clothes and you can hold her." Richard thrust a shapeless gray-green hospital gown into Jake's shaking hands, waiting patiently while he struggled into it. "Now, she's all yours."

For just a split second, Jake could have sworn

there was nothing in the blanket, then he saw the tiny fist curling at its edge. Carefully, like the typical father who thinks babies will break, he lifted away the layers of soft flannel. There wasn't a sound in the room while Richard and Kelly watched as he saw his daughter for the first time. He was as still as he was silent, then with the tip of a finger that seemed huge in contrast, he traced the line of her jaw. It was a full minute more before he lifted his eyes to Kelly's.

"She looks like me," Jake said.

Richard laughed. "I would say that should win the award for understatement of the day. And why be so startled? Who else, other than, Kelly, would she look like?"

"She's perfect," Jake murmured, not aware that Richard had spoken. "You've given me the most precious gift in the world."

Kelly's smile grew brighter even as her eyes filled with happy tears when Jake lay the baby in her arms. His darker head bent over hers as they watched the tiny creature that wiggled and stretched in its pink wrappings.

Only fools never know when they're not needed, and Richard was never that. Offering some excuse that wasn't even heard, he left them.

A soft, sleepy cry broke the quiet that had fallen over the house in the pre-dinner hour. Lily and Lydia had retired to their rooms to dress, while Monroe had busied himself with his routine tasks of the day. Dressed only in her robe, Kelly hurried to answer the call.

The nursery, deliciously pink and yellow, had been a surprise from Lily and Lydia. If either of the two women had thought it strange that it was they who had painted, papered, and decorated in a mad dash the week Nicole had been born, neither ever spoke of it.

"So, sleepyhead, you're awake, are you?" Kelly lifted the tiny child from the bassinet. "You've slept so long, you must be hungry."

She seated herself in the comfortable rocker by the window, deftly adjusted the folds of her robe, and cradled the baby to her. She laughed softly as the tiny mouth eagerly found her breast. With her head bent over the suckling child, she didn't hear the hurried steps.

"Kelly." Jake stopped in the open doorway. "I thought I heard—"

He stood transfixed, his hand gripping the knob, totally captivated by the scene before him. The dim light had turned Kelly's hair a dark, rich gold, but nothing could hide the serene tranquility that lit her face. He had never in his life seen anything as lovely or as moving. Feeling like an intruder, he turned sadly to go.

"Jake?"

It was a slight, husky sound. Had he really heard it or was it only in his heart she spoke? His hand tightened painfully on the knob as he waited.

"Don't go."

"I'm sorry, Kelly, I didn't mean to intrude." He didn't turn. His knuckles were becoming white and still he waited.

"You're not. This is a special time, come share it with us."

"Are you sure?"

"Yes." Her calm assurance swept away his doubts and he joined them.

Kelly made no move to cover herself. Listening to his familiar tread as he crossed the wide expanse of the room, she waited for him to speak. There was only the tiny sounds of the nursing child as he stood over them.

A hesitant finger touched Nicole, then trembled as it traced the line of her cheek to the corner of her mouth. Kelly said nothing as the finger brushed, only slightly, against the sensitive fullness of her breast. It was an enchanted time, not a time for shame or embarrassment.

Jake backed away slowly and sat down opposite them, watching without speaking. When Kelly lifted her head to smile at him, the pride she saw in his eyes swept away her innate shyness.

"She's a hungry tyke, isn't she?" he ventured at last in an unsteady voice.

"Always." She laughed, a magical sound that melted away the last of their tension.

Smiling, Jake leaned back, comfortable for the first time since he had blundered into the room. Unthinking, knowing only that the child had cried, he had rushed in, harried, worn down by the bone wracking tiredness that comes with unrelieved tension. And strangely as he watched this beautiful ritual between mother and child, he felt only contentment. There was only now. Nothing had come before, nothing would come after. There was only this.

His smile deepened, his eyes crinkled, and he chuckled softly. He was bewitched by the strength of the tiny fist that kneaded the smooth swell of Kelly's engorged breast, and laughed aloud at the fierce, urgent rooting as the petal soft mouth searched for a lost nipple.

At the sound of his delighted laughter, Kelly's eyes again met and held with his. Neither realized that the gentle tugging had stopped or that the child had fallen asleep. "Thank you, Kelly," he murmured.

It was a beginning. From that time, it was rare for Jake to miss an evening in the nursery. He adjusted his schedule to match Nicole's, and only at his busiest did he fail to join them. At the end of each day, Kelly waited for a tap on the door. It would be Jake. No one else ventured there at that hour. Tactfully, they were given the privacy due a young couple sharing their first child. From the sharing grew a comfortable friendship they understood, and a deepening love they did not.

"How did your visit with Richard go?" Lily patted the last of her seedlings into its pot then turned to face Kelly.

"He was a bit disturbed that I was two weeks late for my checkup, but other than that everything's terrific. According to Dr. Matthews, I couldn't be in better health. In fact, you can all stop treating me like I'm made of crystal. I could even help you with that planting."

"Good heavens! You know you don't want hands like mine. Poor Nicki would be scratched to death."

"I doubt that. You have the gentlest touch I've ever known, rough hands or no. Nicki loves it when you hold her."

"It's amazing how that child has enchanted us all. Did you see how Lydia's face lit up when you asked her if she could babysit while you were at Richard's office?"

"Mmmm." Kelly nodded. "Speaking of Lydia, I really should get on in and relieve her. She must be tired by now."

"No, give her a few more minutes. She's having the time of her life. She told me earlier that caring for Nicki was like playing with a living doll. And anyway, she's not alone."

"Oh, is David here?"

"No, but haven't you noticed?" Lily made a sweeping gesture with her soil-covered hands. "After years of never knowing where Monroe might be, all of a sudden I know *exactly* where he is. If you ever need the man now, look for Nicki. He won't be far away."

Kelly hid her smile as she leaned against the potting table where Lily was working. For the first time since Kelly had arrived at Caldwell House, Monroe was not two paces behind Lily and for the first time Lily spoke of knowing where he was.

The smile faded as Kelly thought of what her life was going to be like without these dear people. With Richard's glowing report, she had made a definite decision. It was time for her to go.

"There, that's that." Lily dusted off her hands. "I suppose I should start thinking about tonight. I dread it. Carolyn Gallagher's parties are so boring."

"But she's a dear friend and you wouldn't hurt her for the world," Kelly added indulgently.

"Are you sure, dear, that you won't change your mind and come with us?"

"Positive. One exposure to Marsha Gallagher was more than enough."

"Yes, I'm sure it was. Sometimes I wonder how Carolyn could bear to have a fine son like Oscar marry anyone as mean as Marsha." Linking her arm through Kelly's she walked with her from the greenhouse. "Lydia's going to dinner with David, then they plan to drop by the Gallaghers'. That way they can spend as little time as possible in Marsha's company. I'm sure they wouldn't mind if you joined them."

"I wouldn't dream of it," Kelly said adamantly. "I've spent days convincing Lydia to accept this dinner invitation. They certainly don't need me as excess baggage."

"Then I'll leave Monroe with you."

"No, you won't. You know you can't see to drive at night. You're going to the party and Monroe will drive you. Lydia's going out with David. And Nicki and I will have a quiet evening at home. So there's nothing to worry about."

"But dear, I hate to leave you alone. Jake won't be back for three more days. He'll be furious when he finds out we left you alone."

"Lily." Kelly affectionately patted the hand that rested at her elbow. "You're marvelous and I love you, but you worry about the most absurd things. I'll be twenty-six soon and I should think anyone who's reached that ripe old age could take care of herself."

"I don't know . . ." Lily began again, doubtfully.

"But I do." Kelly was firm in her resolve. "In fact you'd better start getting ready now and I should go rescue Lydia from our reigning princess so she can make herself beautiful for David. Run along. I'll see you before you go."

"Good night, sweetheart." Kelly smiled down at the sleeping child. Bathed and powdered, replete and contented, Nicki slept soundly with her knees drawn up beneath her. She only squirmed and stretched slightly as Kelly lovingly kissed the vulnerable curve of her neck, covered by soft downy hair so like Jake's.

Leaving the nursery, Kelly found a certain satisfaction in the silent emptiness of the house. Though none of Jake's family ever imposed on her privacy, she was never truly alone. On an impulse, she decided to make this a special night. She would raid the kitchen for the snacks the cook had left her, cadge a small bottle of wine, and have a private celebration in her room.

She would celebrate the birth of her lovely daughter, and the successful performance that was rapidly coming to an end. If she could create a festive mood, perhaps she could forget for a time that she no longer had reason to stay. She had fulfilled her part of the bargain to the letter, remaining until she was given her medical release following the birth of the baby. Today she had been given that release.

Lingering long in a tub fragrant with Jake's favorite scent, Kelly blanked her mind to all but the deliciously restful heat of the water. Only when it had begun to cool did she step out onto the mat and dry her slender body with a fluffy towel. Tossing it carelessly aside, she walked to the closet. Almost as if it had a mind of its own, her hand fell on the gold gown, the beautiful creation Jake had given her that perfect day on the island.

She stroked the smooth silk, remembering that day. New to a world of so much kindness, she hadn't realized until it was too late that what she felt for Jake was much more than gratitude or even desire. She had loved him even then. She had never worn the gown, but she would tonight, in her silent and private good-bye.

Slipping into it before she could change her mind, she stretched languorously as the shimmering fabric caressed her body. The delicate beige lace hugged the fullness of her breasts and the silk clung to her like liquid gold. She didn't need the mirror to tell her she had never looked so attractive, nor ever would again. With that sixth sense that comes to every woman on rare occasions, she knew she was beautiful.

She had turned out all the lights but the single lamp by the bed and had set her tray of snacks on the bedside table, along with the bottle of wine. She laughed aloud, thinking of how she had pampered herself all evening. Brushing her hair until it glistened, doing her nails, splashing herself with a deliciously wicked cologne, then dressing in a gown designed only for seduction.

"And all you have to share it with is a good book," she reminded herself ruefully.

At the sound of a metallic click, Kelly's breath caught in her throat. Suddenly and intuitively aware that all that had gone before had been a prelude for this moment, she turned slowly, her eyes searching the darkened room.

The door swung open quietly. And as she had known he would be, Jake was there.

"Jake?" His face was in the shadows; she could read nothing from his stance. He stood so utterly still she felt the first stirrings of uneasiness. "I didn't know you were back."

He was silent, a dark, unmoving silhouette in the half light.

"Your mother and Lydia have gone to a party at the Gallaghers'." Stammering, groping, and uncertain beneath his quiet scrutiny, she took one step away from the bed.

His chest rose and fell rapidly with the sudden, raspy breath he drew.

"Nicki's asleep, but I can wake her if you'd like—"

"I've seen her."

Relieved that he had broken his silence, ignoring the curtness of his words, she relaxed. "You must be tired if you've finished your business already. Would you like me to get you something? Some food? A drink?"

"Hush, Kelly." It was a gruff command that startled her into unaccustomed obedience. She looked at him incredulously.

"Be quiet," he repeated, gently this time. "I don't want food. I don't want drink. Just be still and let me look at you."

With the light behind her, she was herself a silhouette. Golden when he had been dark; fragile when he had been strong. The gown served only as a silken web, enhancing with its burnished glow the soft, lean lines of her body. Molding closely to her, the delicate gossamer of the beige lace did little to hide the dusky tint of her nipples. In their new voluptuousness, her breasts strained against the fabric, the cleft becoming an intriguing shadow.

The supple waist, the gentle slope of her narrow hips, the graceful length of her shapely legs . . . She was as he had known she would be. But lovelier, far, far lovelier.

"You're so beautiful." His voice was no longer harsh, but flowed around her like deep, warm velvet. He took a step forward and she could see his eyes as they blazed over her.

Instinctively, she looked down at herself and saw for the first time what he had seen. She had been unconsciously provocative as she stood before him in the lamplight. With its brilliance outlining every curve, every line, there was little left of her he did not see.

She lifted her gaze back to his. She took a deep breath and her full breasts lifted temptingly and the folds of the gown swayed, teasing him with the last mystery of her body. She could feel the hunger in him as his gaze again devoured her. It was then she made her decision. He wanted her; she needed him more than life itself. Tomorrow he would be free, but tonight he could be hers. This much she would have. Tonight would be a memory to cherish.

"I missed you," she murmured, walking slowly to him. As the gown clung then swirled about her, the intoxicating fragrance that would always remind him of her filled his senses.

"I was only gone a little while."

"It didn't matter. I would have missed you if it

had only been for an hour." One more step brought her within his reach.

He slowly drew in a breath and she could tell how desperately he was controlling himself. She slid his tie from his open collar, her fingers trailing lightly across his chest.

"Stop!" he grated through clenched teeth.

"I was only making you more comfortable," she murmured.

"I'm comfortable enough."

"Liar." She laughed softly. "You're never comfortable with a tie."

"Kelly." He captured her hand against his chest. "You're right. I am tired. It's been a long day and I'm not thinking clearly."

"I know." Her free hand stroked the side of his face, then brushed over his tumbled curls, tangling in them at the back of his neck.

A sharp shudder shook his body as he touched her for the first time. His hands covered around her shoulders, his fingers splayed across her bare arms. Suddenly shy, she couldn't hold his gaze. As his thumbs stroked the throbbing pulse on either side of her neck, she memorized the lines of his body, the strong column of his throat, the jut of the lightly bearded jaw. When her eyes met his again, he was waiting for her, reading the tender longing in her wistful smile.

"Are you sure this is what you want, sweetheart?" he asked, his voice low, deep, and trembling with hope. "If it isn't, I can't take much more."

"I'm sure," she whispered as she buried her flaming face in the brawny comfort of his chest.

"Then God forgive me if this is a mistake," he muttered into her hair as his hands drew her closer. Holding her tightly against him, he murmured soothing, nonsensical words. Devastated by his touch, she heard only the rhythmical cadence of his voice.

Gentle hands at her shoulders put her slowly from him. When she started to protest, he quieted her with a finger against her quivering lips.

"Shhh, sweetheart, don't rush it. Let's take it slow and easy. There's no hurry."

The finger left her lips to trace the contours of her face and throat, pausing at the hollow where her heart pounded its mad beat, then trailed across the smooth curve of her breast. Defeated in his quest by the lacy scallops of the gown, he did not transgress, but followed its path to the vee that dipped low between her breasts. Then he cupped her breasts, lifted them, and bent to pay homage with his lips. His tongue traced the delicate roughness of the nipple beneath the lace. An electric sweetness rippled in her blood as he tugged gently, taking her into the heat of his mouth.

His hands brushed across her shoulders and the golden straps fell away. The faithful lace of the bodice defied gravity for an instant, then it too fell away, unveiling the enticing fullness of her breasts. The gown clung once more at her waist, only to slip again slowly, silk against silk, until it lay like a pool of burnished moonbeams about her feet. Kelly felt no shame as Jake saw for the first time the new, lush shapeliness of her body.

"So soft, so lovely," he muttered as he touched the bareness revealed to his ravenous eyes.

Kelly reveled in the ardent tenderness of his hands on her body, welcomed the strength of his embrace when he drew her close. Tilting her face to his, he kissed her. A long, slow, sweet kiss that left her breathless, yet strangely bereft. Her arms slipped about him and her hands pressed against his bare back. She had no memory of him taking off his shirt. She arched against him and the dark, sweet hunger that had been his constant source of quiet insanity became a raging force since he had lifted her from the floor of her apartment.

With a ragged groan, he swept her from her feet and moved blindly to the bed. He sat on its edge, cradling her on his knees, learning the shape of her with his lips. Again his mouth took hers as he filled one hand with her golden curls, holding her a willing captive for his kiss. Lightly first, then again slowly, then deeper, as she opened to the inevitable fulfillment, his tongue learned the sweet depths of her mouth.

She leaned into his embrace, yielding herself to him, meeting his hunger with her own. He trembled as her arms drew him ever closer, her bare breasts crushed against his chest.

"Now, Kelly, now." His eyes had darkened to blue-black. Something untamed flickered in their depths before her buried his lips in her throat.

"Yes, now," she pleaded as the last vestige of reality slipped away as easily as the gown had from her body.

He eased her down on the dark velvet coverlet, then impatiently freed himself from the encumbrance of his clothing. Kelly was aware, as never before, of his body. Each lithe and graceful move bespoke beauty and she knew no man had ever been more masculine or more virile. He carelessly tossed aside the last of his garments and stood over her, a look of rapt admiration on his face. The glitter in his eye told her that she was indeed feminine and desirable, the perfect counterpart of his maleness. Her eager need matched his and she was grateful when he finally lay by her side.

Leaning over her, Jake found himself by turns anxious and hesitant. The consummation he had dreamed of for so long was at hand, yet he needed to prolong the sweetness of the moment. With soft, sweeping gestures, he caressed her, his fingers tracing hungrily over her face, her shoulders. His palm lingered at the inviting crest of one breast, then stroked downward across her smooth skin to circle tantalizingly about her navel. Then he replaced his hand with his lips and his tongue savored the fragrance of the tiny well as his hand wandered lower. He brushed only lightly across her silken curls before exploring the rounded contour of her hip. With agonizing slowness his fingers glided over the flat plane of her thighs, coming to rest at last in the most loving of caresses at the quintessence of her femininity. At her restive stirring, he lifted his head, drawing back to seek and learn again every part of her.

At his first touch, Kelly's breast grew firm and turgid, responding to Jake's gentle tugging as it did to Nicki's. As he watched the bewitching play of lights and shadows that sculptured her body, changing with every halting breath, a single droplet formed at her nipple. Fascinated, he brushed it away, hardly aware of Kelly's soft sigh when he stroked the tender tip. Another drop welled to take its place, shimmering against the dusky crest with the opalescence of a pearl.

Slowly, mesmerized by the sheer wonder, he lowered his head and swept the drop away with his tongue. Sighing again, Kelly whispered a plea, needing him.

His breath tantalized her skin once more as he caressed the taut areola. Then, as slowly as it had descended, his head lifted until his eyes met Kelly's.

"I'm tempted to take what is my daughter's," he said, his voice itself a gentle caress. "Instead I will take what is mine."

Eyes shining, Kelly welcomed him. Her last fleeting thought was that there could be no turning back. It was far too late. All her bridges were burned, but it didn't matter. Tonight was hers. Tomorrow she would set him free.

As her body lifted to receive him she knew for the first time in her life a sense of completeness, a sense of self. Nicki had been conceived in an act of caring. This, this beautiful God-given moment when her body joined with Jake's was an act of love. Jake, who filled her world, her life, and her body with the most exquisite joy, was hers. Would always be hers in that secret part of her heart where treasures were kept. And because of him, she would forever be complete.

As separate beings, yet only one, they moved together in love. Taking by giving, conquering by yielding; fiercely gentle, then gently fierce. Silently, communicating only by tender kiss and loving caress, they came shatteringly to the place that was theirs alone. Only her cry, a soft murmuring sound, broke the hush of the dimly lit room.

For the space of a heartbeat Jake poised above her, his eyes silver-blue. In a most natural gesture, he brushed back her tousled hair from her face. Kissing first one eye closed and then the other, he whispered, "My sweet Kelly, was there ever such a woman as you?"

Lazily, moving as in a dream, he turned to his side, drawing her with him, bodies melding. Tenderly, he tucked her head next to his heart, chuckling as she nestled into his warmth like a tiny kitten. Then quietly, sated and happy, they drifted together into sleep.

Hours later, bodies entwined amid a tangle of covers, Jake woke her with a caress. Answering her soft pleading cries he made love to her slowly, gently, more wonderfully than before.

Afterward, fulfilled and drowsily content, more asleep than awake, she nearly destroyed him. The fire in his heart turned to ice with her whispery murmur.

"Freedom for a memory. I can go now. I have my memory." Then, inexplicably, snuffing out the last tiny but stubborn hope that still flickered and might have warmed his heart, she spoke a single word. The name of he who had nothing yet everything to do with this moment.

". . . Scott."

And Jake's destruction was complete.

Ten

"Good morning." Kelly stood in the archway that led to the breakfast room, surveying the table before her. Jake's place was empty.

"Good morning. Did you sleep well?" Lily smiled in secret satisfaction at the happiness on Kelly's face.

"Mrs. Jake." Monroe held her chair. His lips, still the perfect expressionless line of the perfect servant, lifted slightly for an uncontrollable instant in appreciation of her contented aura of a woman well loved.

"Did Jake say what time he would be back from the office today?" Kelly could hardly contain her lilting eagerness. When she had thought to steal a memory, she had instead been given paradise. Jake had turned her world on its axis and everything had changed. Surely a perfect interlude, so fragilely beautiful must mean something. Surely . . .

". . . surely you knew."

"No! I mean, I beg your pardon?" Kelly stammered, drawing herself back to the present, ominously reluctant to hear.

"I said, my dear, that Jake isn't here. He left earlier for Savannah." Lily laid down her fork to study Kelly with a puzzled gaze. Then she asked gently, "You did know, didn't you, Kelly?"

"Yes. Yes, of course I knew." The bewildered lie was dust on her tongue as dark premonition lacerated newfound serenity. Savannah, and he hadn't bothered to say good-bye. Even after last night. *What have I done?*

"Perhaps you were too tired to understand when he said good-bye." Soothing words, but useless.

"That must be what happened." Seizing on any excuse, Kelly roused herself from the raw pain, tried to hide her distress, and failed miserably.

"I shouldn't think that the two of you spent the only night you had the house alone together discussing his departure," Lily teased, striving to bring back the smile that had been so radiant only seconds ago. A mechanical nod was her only answer.

"Mrs. Jake would like a fresh cup of coffee." Monroe hovered, making no attempt to hide his concern at the sudden and startling change. An abrupt shake of her head was her first unthinking rebuff of his kind ministrations.

"Kelly," Lily said quietly, "he left you a note on his desk."

"A . . . a note?"

"Run along, dear," Lily urged. "Of course you want to read it. I should have mentioned it earlier."

Kelly sprang up from the table and left the room in clumsy haste. As Lily has said, there was an envelope lying on the bare surface of his desk, her name scrawled across it in his bold hand. With trembling hands, she tore it open, puzzled by the keys that slipped with a clatter to the desk. Drawing out the single sheet, she began to read, stopped, brushed away a solitary tear, then read again. Twice more she read the cold, dispassionate words.

Kelly,
　　Our bargain is at an end. Please consider the beach house yours for as long as you wish. I will make our excuses to Mother when I return.
　　Thank you for a job well done.

　　　　　　　　　　　　　　　　　Jake

There were no more tears. Her eyes were hot and dry as she faced the desolation of her future. From the time Jake had come into her life, she had lived a fairy tale existence. In place of a lonely life of solitude, she had been given a handsome husband, a perfect child, and the first real family she had ever known. Now the enchantment had come to an end.

Kelly crumpled the distant, expressionless note in her shaking fist. Last night might never have happened. Was it possible that the Jake who had written this and the Jake who had loved her so passionately could be the same man? Had he, too, been saying good-bye? Smoothing the crumpled page, she read the message again, although already it was carved into the deepest recesses of her mind.

"Thank you for a job well done," she murmured as a bitter, self-mocking smile curled her lips. Unconsciously, she straightened her shoulders, steeling herself to deal with one more loss, the most devastating yet.

Reaching deeply into a well of inner strength she had never known she possessed, Kelly survived. She made her plans as she went about her daily routine, talking with Lily and Lydia, jousting with Monroe, and caring for Nicki.

Delving even deeper into that well, she sat serenely while a cold, curt Jake gathered the family in the library and explained that, despite their every effort, their marriage had failed again. She managed to project an air of sad acceptance as he assured the others there was no chance for reconciliation. This time the marriage was truly at an end. She listened as he discussed her plans to live for a while at the beach and agreed with his insistence that they should all feel free to visit as often as they could.

Kelly had been badly in error when she had protested that she was not an actress. Hers was the performance of a lifetime. She was so immersed in it that her eyes only looked inward, never seeing the pain that ravaged Jake. She did not see how he watched her hungrily, hoping for some sign that this separation was not what she wished. Nor did she hear how he cursed himself for that hope. She could not know how often he called himself fool for wanting a woman who spoke another man's name in the aftermath of ecstacy. Fool he might be, but he did watch and he did hope, waiting for a sign that never came. Jake, an audience of one, blinded by a performance that convinced only one.

There is in the mind the power to blank out and to soften the unbearable until one garners strength. It was this power that allowed Kelly to move in an aura of quiet calm, leaving the inevitable grieving for a private time. Each day she summoned that inner strength and power, always fearful that this time it would fail her. But she never faltered.

Only once did her iron will nearly crumble. She rarely had seen Jake since his return from Savannah and never alone, until the evening she met him in the dimly lit hallway outside his study. When she would have passed him by silently, his hand closed tightly around her wrist, halting her. He waited, looming over her like a specter, as time stretched between them. Only the rasp of his breathing rippled the dark quiet.

"Is it so important to you?" Low and guttural, made harsh by pain, his voice assaulted her. "Must you have this freedom you speak of?"

"Yes," she hissed defiantly, ignoring the deadening of her hand as his fingers cut into the flesh. "Freedom is important to every living thing. Nothing should be held an unwilling captive." Kelly stopped short, realizing she dared not say more. Only after he released her did she notice the ache from his paralyzing grip.

Jake stood unmoving, not touching her again, devouring her with eyes that held a hopeless resignation. In an unusually awkward move, he turned away abruptly. She didn't dare look up until she heard the study door close behind him. Only then did she allow herself to slump wearily against the wall, stroking her bruised wrist with her tongue. Here, blended with a hint of alcohol, was the intoxicating essence of Jake.

Dry eyed, she whispered to the closed door, "Not my freedom, darling, yours."

Hurriedly she left the hall, not hearing the chime

of crystal against crystal as a tormented man tried once more to drink himself into insensibility.

By the day of her departure, the hollow victory was hers. Jake had no concept of the deep love that was his and would always be his alone. She had known, instinctively, that should he realize her love, he would in sympathy give her more of himself. Kelly wanted all that Jake could give, but not out of pity. Never pity! No, he must see her exactly as he did, a young woman embarking on the rest of her life. To that end, her bags were packed and waiting.

On this beautiful, sunlit day, everything was in readiness. The car was loaded, Nicole was dressed, Lily, Lydia, and Monroe were waiting to say good-bye. There was nothing more to do, yet she lingered in the room she had shared with Jake, storing up memories to help make bearable the days to come. She stood at the window staring at the river as it meandered lazily past the house. She would miss even this, a view that had given her long hours of pleasure.

"Are you ready?" She didn't turn from the window at the sound of his voice.

"Yes."

"Do you have everything you need?"

"Everything." She nodded absently, fighting the tight constriction in her throat. "You've been more than generous."

"Dammit, Kelly!"

"Jake." They spoke at once, then were both silent. As the excruciating void yawned between them, she turned to face him, barely stifling her shock at his evident exhaustion. Since that evening in the hallway she had seen even less of him. He spent his days at the office, his nights in the study, and he slept God knows where.

"About the divorce—"

"Don't concern yourself, Kelly," he interrupted curtly.

"We really should discuss it."

"No!" The word was muttered through grim,

unrelenting lips. "Why don't you go down now? They're waiting for you."

He left her, more alone than she had ever been. It wasn't until she heard the familiar closing of the study door that she made her way down to Lily and Lydia. Monroe, as usual, waited one pace away. Kelly paused only a fraction of a second before going into Lily's open arms.

"We'll miss you," Lily said, "but the island's such a short drive, we can see you often. We might even make nuisances of ourselves."

"Never! Come as often as you like."

"And will you visit us, dear?"

"Perhaps it wouldn't be a good idea." Kelly cleared away the persistent, aching lump that had closed her throat again. "Jake might not approve."

"Fiddlesticks! This will always be your home and Jake knows it."

"Thank you, Lily. I can't tell you how much that means to me." A quick kiss on the powdered cheek, a tight hug, and Kelly moved away.

"Lydia." She took the hand the other woman offered. It was no longer so frail and thin, and roses bloomed in the face that smiled far more often than it had before. "You will keep me up to date on your music?"

"You can count on it. I'll probably be visiting you as often as Lily. You won't mind if David comes, will you?"

"I'd like it. He's been a good friend." Only Monroe was left. Kelly took the few steps to where he waited away from the group, but very much a part of it. Her hand was unsteady as she touched his arm.

"Who will be around to bully me now?" She tried to tease, but her voice broke dreadfully on the words. She blinked hard, then continued bravely. "Without you, I probably wouldn't have remembered to eat or rest properly. Thank you for taking such good care of me."

"It was always my pleasure, Mrs. Jake." As he took her hand in his and bent to place a courtly kiss on her fingers, Kelly could have sworn she saw a hint of tears.

An awkward pause lengthened torturously. Kelly couldn't keep her eyes from straying to the study door. It remained firmly closed as it had for days. Jake would not say good-bye.

"Mrs. Jake." Monroe's kindly voice calmed the wild pain that clawed through her. "Miss Nicole is waiting in the car."

"Yes, of course, Monroe." It was time to go.

Behind the closed doors of the study, Jake waited and watched, hidden by the sheer curtain that covered the window. In his hand was a glass freshly filled with Scotch, but he was oblivious to all but Kelly as she moved down the walk. His gaze clung hungrily to her, catching a glimpse of her face when she turned toward the house one last time. She stood motionless for an eternity, but a new kindling hope died as she stepped quickly to the waiting car.

Long after the sleek Mercedes had disappeared, he listened to its fading rumble. When there was only silence, his face twisted with pain.

She's gone! Two words, consigning him to hell. With a low, savage snarl, he spun from the window. In a graceful arc, the glass flew from his hand and splintered into a myriad of diamondlike pieces against the stone fireplace.

"Why, Kelly?"

"There now. All done." Lily knelt on the pathway that led from the lawn to the beach. "By the time warm weather really gets here, these should be blooming nicely.

"Should I talk to them?" Kelly laughed as she sat on the terrace taking advantage of the warm April day. Nicki had just been fed and slept in a pram nearby.

"Of course you should. Plants are like people. They thrive on love. But a little fertilizer might do just as much." Lily grinned.

"I'll pretend I didn't hear that."

"Right. It was out of character, wasn't it?" Resting on her haunches, Lily adjusted her hat then broached a painful subject, the real reason for her visit. "Speaking of acting out of character, have you heard from Jake?"

"No. Not a word in all these weeks." Kelly had hoped for a long while that she would hear something. Every day was spent waiting for a call, a letter, or a visit, but none ever came. Curiously, neither had there been any word of the divorce. In time she had learned to be calm when there was a knock at the door or the phone rang. Jake had put her from his mind and life, and she knew that if she meant to survive, she must do the same.

"But the roses!" Lily protested. "Surely they meant something."

"They were for Nicki. He sent them the day she was three months old."

"Now, don't tell me he didn't send any sort of message with them." Her red curls bobbed as she spoke emphatically.

"There was a message, but not for me. He wrote a lovely note saying he wanted to be the first man in Nicki's life to send her red roses."

"Humph! That's a beautiful thought, but what good is it really? Nicki needs him, not red roses."

"He's never even asked to see her." The despair Kelly thought she had under control started to grow.

"Something's wrong," Lily insisted. "This isn't like Jake at all. He's always had a strong sense of responsibility. In fact, he carried Scott's burdens as well as his own." She paused to smile at Kelly. "Jake doesn't realize that I've always known about Scott's transgressions. He's tried to protect me from them the same way he's protected Lydia from Scott's infidelity. But a mother knows these things, intuitively."

"What!" A sudden fear that Lily was saying much more blanched Kelly's face. "What do you mean?"

"Nothing really." The older woman graciously eased Kelly's mind. "But after years of knowing and understanding my son, I find myself faced with a stranger. He doesn't eat or sleep, and when we try to get him to rest, he snarls at us like a wounded bear. It's nothing for him to work sixteen hours a day. He's forgotten that there's a world out here. And worse, he's shamefully neglecting his daughter."

"Neither of us lacks for anything," Kelly interjected mildly. "He's seen to that."

"That's where you're wrong. Material things can't take the place of a father. Since Jake lost his own father so young he should know that better than most." It was a firm pronouncement that allowed no argument.

"Can't you get him to slow down?" Kelly pleaded, her face ashen in the bright sunlight. "He'll make himself sick."

"He's already sick, Kelly. Sick at heart. He lives every day in quiet desperation. It's frightening. Sometimes I wonder if he'll survive." Lily watched regretfully as the mask of control slipped irrevocably from Kelly's pale features. It was painful to see, but this was a very necessary part of her plan. Now for the next step in the tangled web she was unweaving.

Rising like a young girl, she dusted off her hands. "It's getting late. I really must be going. Lydia is expecting David for dinner. Monroe? Monroe? Where is that man?"

"Here, Madame."

There was a distant drumming of thunder as Jake opened and closed the door quietly. Lightning flashed, its eerie glow throwing his face into stark relief. Tiny drops of rain glistened on his hair and shoulders as, careful to make little noise, he shrugged out of his wet coat.

"Jake."

"Mother! What on earth are you doing up at this hour? It's after three."

"I waited up to speak to you."

"Something's wrong." He was instantly taut, his nerves ragged. "It's Kelly."

"Yes." She offered the one word, letting his tired imagination run the spectrum. As with Kelly, she hated what she was doing. But, if the end results were what she hoped, perhaps she would be forgiven.

"Is she hurt? Ill? Tell me, Mother."

"Neither," Lily placated, taking his arm. "Come into the library. We can talk there without disturbing Lydia and Monroe." Once in that room, she took her time, drawing him with slow precision to the breaking point. From her seat, she watched as he paced. "I was with Kelly today and she doesn't look well." Steadfastly ignoring his agonized groan and hardening her tender heart, she continued with her attack. "She isn't sleeping, she isn't eating. Perhaps she isn't ill yet, but it's only a matter of time. But the worst part is that she's so very tense. I'm afraid all this will transfer to Nicki. Then both of them—Jake! Where are you going?"

"To Kelly!"

"No!" Lily left her chair so rapidly it tipped over with a crash.

"I have to go." He raked his hands through his hair impatiently and the deep slashes by his mouth grew more pronounced and grimmer.

"Be reasonable, Jake." Lily patted his hand. "By now she will have finally fallen asleep. Do you really want to disturb her? Wait. Maybe in a day or two you can go over to see how she is."

"A day or two, hell!" he growled, irritated even as he recognized the wisdom of her words. He wouldn't wait a day or two. He couldn't. First thing tomorrow he would go to the island.

"Why don't you get some rest?" his mother prodded gently. "You can't be of much help to Kelly if you're exhausted too."

"I suppose you're right." His shoulders slumped in weariness as he stooped to kiss her cheek. "Good night, Mother."

Lily listened to his slow, measured tread climbing the stairs. "I hope I've done the right thing," she murmured as she stroked the velvety green leaves of the

African violet by her side. "What else could I do, Margaret? They were both so stubborn. Someone had to end this foolish separation."

In the soft mist of an early evening rain, lights glittered over wet pavement. A sharp curve, the desperate screech of tormented tires, in slow motion a car flew into the darkening sky. It hung suspended endlessly. A jagged bolt of lightning split heaven and earth. Thunder rumbled, threatened, faded away. Darkness obscured.

Agony . . . the demented scream of twisted metal skidding over stone . . . the crash of battered trees . . . the crackle of hungry flames . . . Silence.

Running footsteps, frantic and afraid. Alone in the darkness. Branches, sinister black and skeletal, lashed viciously. Briers clawed savagely, tangling in his hair. Long ropes of brambles clutched at his clothing, winding snakelike about his legs, holding him captive. He struggled futilely, again and again, against the shackling. Exhausted and powerless, caught in the reptilian coil, he watched with horror as flames began their deadly dance. Their flickering lights painted patterns of evil across the sweet, still face and golden curls.

"Kelly!"

The anguished cry was ripped from his throat as Jake bolted upright, trembling, bathed in the cold, acrid sweat of terror. Confused and disoriented, he was slow to realize the harsh madness of the dream had faded. In its aftermath he was left with a reality as painful. He ached with need as he watched the first gray light of dawn filter through the shuttered doors. Long shadows filled the room. A room that was empty without Kelly.

He would go to her. She needed him.

The drabness of early dawn had given way to fiery red as Jake roared down the last winding road to the beach house. Only the muffled report of his car door disturbed the tranquility that lay lightly over the spring morning. Hardly aware that he held it, he took with him the long, slender package he found on the car seat. Its card bore only Kelly's name in his mother's spidery script.

There was no answer to his quiet tap. Impatient, he used his key. If she was still asleep, he wouldn't wake her. He could wait. Treading softly through the house, he checked the bedrooms. Nicki slept in the smaller one, warm and pink with her knees tucked under her, her bottom in the air. His unsteady fingers hovered near her smooth cheek, needing to touch it. He had missed her.

The second bedroom was empty, and the third. Where was Kelly? Mindlessly he set the box on a low table. The hand he ran over his tired eyes shook until he closed it into a tight fist. Where was Kelly?

He became aware of sounds of the surf, rough now because of the recent storm. In his agitation, he hadn't noticed that the louvered doors stood open. The soft, unnaturally balmy air of mid-April kissed his face as it crept into the bedroom. In quick, urgent strides he walked out onto the balcony.

Kelly stood at the water's edge. Waves played about her feet, wetting her gown, molding it to her as they splashed. The wind tousled her hair into inviting disarray. As she stared at the water that sparkled in the fully risen sun, she was herself bathed in—

"Sunshine." It was a low cry, lost in the pounding of the surf, but she heard. Turning slowly, she faced him.

He had come. Wondrously, Jake, her delight and her torment, was here. The light was unkind to him, carving every tired line deeper, emphasizing his haggard pallor. The smile that had so often curved his lips had been replaced by a grim remoteness. With sudden clarity, she understood his unnatural despondency. Jake was suffering, and whatever the reason, Kelly knew with an inexplicable certainty that she was the key. Only she could offer the succor he must have. With this intuitive knowledge and because she loved him, she would heal him. Sparing no thought to the sadness that might lie in her future, her decision made, she walked toward him. The smile on her lips was tender beyond belief.

"She's coming to me." The thought rocketed through his brain in excruciating recognition. "Not to Scott's brother, not to the guardian of her child, but to me. She's coming to me." He repeated it in a litany, his whisper was caught and tossed away by the wind.

Nothing could take away the love that now blazed in the aching void of his life. As he moved at last to meet her, the band of ice that had held his heart these many weeks shattered and fell away. The first real smile he had known in a long time danced across his face as he began to run.

He swept her into his arms. Mindless of the wet gown, he held her to him, murmuring disjointed phrases only she could understand, punctuating each with a kiss. "I dreamed . . . I was so worried . . . Mother said . . . not sleeping . . . not eating . . . so thin . . . Sweetheart . . . I missed you . . . need you."

Kelly linked her hands behind his neck, meeting kiss with kiss, murmuring between his words. "You came . . . I wished . . . I dreamed . . . I prayed . . . and you came."

"I'll always come when you need me."

"I know." She nodded, then shivered in delight at his dark look of desire.

"You're cold!" he scolded, striding to the house. He had her stripped of her wet gown and sitting on the bed wrapped in a warm blanket before he spoke again. "What were you doing out in the morning air dressed only in your nightgown?"

"I was wishing for you." Her innocent face raised to his swept his intent to chastise.

"I'm here, beloved." He gathered her into the loving shelter of his arms.

"Beloved?" Kelly's mind reeled at the endearment, leaving her breathless and so afraid to believe.

"Yes. Beloved," he murmured in a growl, his breath stirring her hair. Then with agonizing slowness, he tilted her head against his shoulder. Truth raged in his eyes. "Surely you've known from the first that I love you."

She shook her head as she searched his face carefully. It was there, the look that had tormented her. How often had she thought she would sell her soul to understand that look? Now she recognized it. Jake loved her, and she would gladly *give* him her soul for that love. Delicious desire shimmered through her. He was hers! "Jake, I—"

"Shhh." He stopped her with a gentle finger against her lips. "I love you and I'll never let you leave me again. You and Nicki need me. It's enough for now."

"No!" The blanket fell from her shoulders as she lifted her arms and cupped his face between her hands. Her fingertips lightly brushed a stray lock of hair from his temple. Amber eyes that blazed with a love of her own met and held the dark, passionate blue of his. "It's not enough. For years you've protected those you care for, stepping aside for Scott until it became a way of life. It's past time that you got what *you* want. Tell me, Jake"—Kelly's grip tightened in his hair as she demanded his answer—"what is it you want from me?"

His gaze raked over the naked loveliness of her breasts as the blanket dipped further down her body. Almost angrily he crushed her to him, burying his lips in the tender flesh of her throat in an urgent need to possess. Kelly met his demands with gentle abandon. It was only when she felt a shudder quake through him that she drew away.

"Tell me!" she commanded fiercely. "Tell me, now."

His eyes closed, his forehead touched hers lightly, and the rusty sound of his words made her life complete. "I want you, Kelly. I want all the love you could ever give a man to be mine. Can you love, me, Sunshine?"

"Jason Caldwell," she sighed, cradling his head to her breasts. "I *do* love you. I *have* loved you since the night you stood in the door of my apartment call-

ing me Miss O'Brian. I will *always* love you. I have
never loved another man and I never will."

Jake grew utterly still. Not by so much as a flicker
of one muscle did he betray his astonishment. Seconds ticked slowly into minutes before he responded
in a strangled voice.

"Don't, sweetheart." He shook his head in denial,
his chest heaving with the painful effort of speech.
"You'll be damning me to a lifetime in hell if you say
that and don't mean it."

"Hush." Kelly rose to her knees, shrugging aside
the cumbersome blanket in irritation. Clasping his
head again between her hands, she stared him fully
in the face. "Look at me. Look! And I dare you to deny
what you see."

Slowly, fearfully, Jake's eyes searched hers and
found them to be a true mirror of her heart. He had
his answer. With a low moan he drew her bare body to
his. With lips that worshiped, he paid homage to her.
When he leaned her back against the pillows her arms
locked about his neck, drawing him with her. Anxious for him, she writhed beneath every new and
deliberate caress, her body an inferno at his touch.
The taut peaks of her breasts burned until he soothed
them with his lips and tongue. As his mouth met hers
in a deep, hungry kiss, she opened to him, caressing
as he caressed. His hands drew her to him and she
arched to meet his possession with the cry of truth on
her lips.

"I love you."

It was as it had been before, but far more won-
drous. A celebration of the love that had always been,
known now and fully shared. His given as hers,
unreservedly and forever. Their bodies merged and
were as one, declaring over and again the pledge of a
lifetime.

At the first urgent joining, there was the still,
hushed savoring of a moment that would never come
again, no matter how many times they loved. It was
the poignant discovery that each had come home.
Never again to be one alone, but always two together.

Whether joined as now or apart, Jake was Kelly's world, as she was his. His murmured "I love you" blended with hers, and the anguish of the past months disappeared as words ceased to matter.

Yet in this enchanged time, with memories of Jake as man and lover etched vividly in her heart, Kelly sensed a smoldering restraint. Too eager for him and far too greedy to accept anything but the total wealth of his passion, she asked a silent question.

As true lovers often do, he understood the unspoken thought far better than eloquent words. "You're so little. I love you so much. I'm afraid."

"You won't hurt me, Jake. You couldn't, not with your love." Her hands slid lovingly over broad shoulders, down his muscular back to lean flanks, drawing him closer, compelling him to believe. "I need your strength as well as your gentleness."

"Kelly." Her name was a prayer on his lips as he complied with her quiet demands. There was no more constraint between them, nor would there ever be.

Long after Jake slept heavily by her side with his hand curved possessively around her breast, Kelly lay watching him. She relearned his hard, lean features. An obvious weight loss had given a craggier cut to his jaw, and sharp lines of fatigue had cut deep furrows across his broad forehead. Yet even as he slept, some of the harshness softened. She vowed to wipe the last of the tension from him. Curling into him with her head nestled under his chin, her fingers tangled in the coarse hair of his chest, and soothed by the rhythm of his even breathing, she drifted into the first contented sleep she had known in weeks.

Kelly slipped quietly from the bed as sunlight dappled the room with the brightness of midday. She tiptoed to the doors, intending to close the shutters.

"Good morning, sweetheart."

"I thought you were asleep." She whirled to smile at him.

"Nope. But I am lonely." He opened his arms, laughing as she flew into them.

"Did you sleep well? You were so tired this morning, I was afraid Nicki and I would disturb you."

"You didn't sleep?"

"Ummm. Twice." She snuggled down beside him, leaning against his chest. With one hand propped over the other and her chin resting on them, she studied him intently. "I slept after you loved me, then again after Nicki had her breakfast."

He laughed ruefully. "I must have been sleeping soundly. I didn't hear a thing."

"Well, considering that I'm her breakfast, there's not much noise involved, unless she gets impatient."

"I think I'd like to have you for breakfast." His eyes had grown dark with the familiar passion as his hands stroked the softness of her hip.

"Be my guest, Mr. Caldwell." She slid up his body to kiss his mouth fiercely, rolling as she kissed him, drawing his body with her. Feeling his welcome weight and fully aware of his arousal, she was startled when he tensed and drew away.

"Will you tell me about Scott?" It was a tortured whisper, torn between need and dread.

His intensity startled her. She looked at his tight, closed face and realized that it was past time that he knew. She hesitated as one small lingering doubt crossed her mind. They loved so completely, could she make him understand the heartrending loneliness that had driven her to settle for less? As quickly as the thought was formed, she knew her answer. Yes, he would understand and because he loved her, he would forgive.

"It's not a very long story, nor a very pretty one. I met Scott while I was filling in at Nick's for a week. Scott was sick and drinking heavily then. For some reason after that he dropped in whenever I was around. He seemed to depend on me to stay sober. I was lonely and he said he needed me. When he asked me to marry him, I agreed."

"Just like that? Short and to the point. You never loved him?"

"No." She looked him squarely in the face, completely steady and assured. "It was true when I said I'd never loved any man but you."

"You called his name."

"Yes." Kelly remembered and she understood. "I was letting go of a hate I never knew I felt, and I blessed him."

"For Nicki?" His hoarse voice was unsteady.

"No." She shook her head, her gaze never leaving him. "For you."

Jake stared at her with that wild, untamed light glowing in the depths of his eyes and Kelly longed to go into his arms. But a long, angry wail broke the golden enchantment of their moment. The bright glitter dimmed to a soft glow as Jake chuckled.

"It sounds as if someone else has breakfast on her mind."

"Except for her, it's lunch. Why don't you take a shower while I see to her, then I'll make you a meal."

"Sounds good, but I'd like to join the two of you, if you don't mind. I've missed that."

"I don't mind." She smiled. "Nicki's missed you as much as I."

Nicki had been bathed and powdered and was ravenously hungry by the time Jake emerged from his shower. Kelly had just slipped her robe from her shoulders and placed the child at her breast when he sat beside her. Delighted with the antics of the hungry child, he watched in fascination as if it were the first time he had seen her nuzzle fiercely as she groped for the nipple lost in her strong suckling. Laughing, he teased as she pushed and kneaded, most indignantly. He called her tiger and stroked her cheek.

"This was the vision I carried with me when we were apart. It's still the most beautiful thing I've ever seen."

"Then you've forgiven me for marrying Scott without love?"

"What's there to forgive? You did exactly as I had been doing all my life. From the day when we were six years old and I discovered how Scott resented that I had the family name and he the reversal, I gave in to him. In some childish way I was trying to make it up to him. After that, he never seemed to grow up. I should have tried to stop his marriage to Lydia, but I kept hoping she could help him."

"Lydia said he was never cruel to her," Kelly said.

"He wouldn't be, not consciously, only by omission. Scott simply couldn't cope. That's why he couldn't face Lydia's being confined to a wheelchair. He ran from one disaster straight into your arms, creating another. Even then he hadn't learned from his mistakes. When he returned to Lydia, he was no better."

"You were always his source of strength and courage, weren't you?" Kelly could at last understand the poor, misguided Scott. "He was looking for another Jake when he found me."

"That's not very flattering to you," Jake said shortly.

"I think it is. You didn't hurt him, you know. If you hadn't been there he would have leaned on someone else. You can't blame yourself for the things he did."

"Maybe not." He was obviously unconvinced by her logic. Nicki squirmed, making a contented sound. He smiled down at her. "Let me put her to bed. Why don't you take your shower while I rummage in the kitchen for the makings of an omelet."

"A bargain. You get out the ingredients and I'll make you an omelet that will make you forget your troubles."

"I don't have any troubles, at least not anymore." He grinned as he took the baby from her. "Now scoot or I'll give you a shower myself."

"Promises, promises." Kelly laughed as she disappeared into the bathroom. When she was finished he was waiting for her, sitting on the bed. She hadn't bothered with her robe, but had tucked a towel across her breasts. She was flushed from the heat of the water and a blush added its color when she saw his face.

"You're the only woman I know who's so pretty in a towel."

"And how many women do you know who dress in towels?" The smile she gave him was of sheer adoration and total possession.

"None but you," he admitted.

"Then how can you say I'm prettiest?"

"Because I have eyes. Come here. I have something for you. Mother sent it."

Kelly broke the ribbons that tied the box, then lifted from its moist wrappings a beautiful yellow rose. There was a card attached to its stem.

Dear children,

I hope that by the time you think to read this you won't need its advice. Kelly, you are now the red chrysanthemum. From slighted love of the yellow, to the truth of white, you have become the beautiful *I love* of the red. Only you can make Jake the complete cedar . . . strong, incorruptible, *I live for thee.*

And he will live for you, Kelly, if you will let him. Forgive the past, recognize the gift you've been given. Follow the message of this rose. Speak low when you speak love.

Forgive a meddling old woman,

Lily

"She knows! Just yesterday she spoke of a mother's intuition." Kelly covered her stricken face with her hands. "What must she think of me?"

"She loves you as I do." He drew her down to his lap, smoothing her hair. "I suspect she knew before I did all the things I was afraid to admit. Did you know that the first time I saw you I was angry with you?"

Kelly could only shake her head and snuggle closer against him.

"Furious might be a better word. I know now that it was because I thought you loved Scott and I wanted it to be me. For once I wanted *his* woman. I was even afraid to admit aloud that I needed your love for fear I could never have it. Have you any idea how happy it made me to hear you say you never loved him?"

"Will you be furious with Nicki, too, because she's his child?"

"No. Because she's not. She's mine. I think of you both as Scott's farewell gift to me."

"And when we have other children?" Kelly ached with pent-up emotion, the co-mingling of fear and elation.

He chuckled. "You should hear Richard on that subject."

"Richard?" Her eyes widened in surprise. "What does he have to do with this?"

"If you will remember, love, we shared a rather special night a few weeks ago. In the heat of the moment, I didn't exactly, ahh, practice common sense. Since then I've been half out of my mind for fear that you might be pregnant again. When I discussed the possibility with him, he reminded me that you'd gotten pregnant when using a contraceptive before, then proceeded to call me every kind of fool in the book, and invented a few as well."

"Then you don't want children?"

"Yes, I do, but not as the result of blind desperation. I've already tried to tie you to me with lies and that's bad enough."

"Lies?" Kelly faltered, confusion adding to the kaleidoscope of wild sensations that were assaulting her.

"Sweetheart, there was no trust fund, no inheritance clause. They were all lies, invented to bind you to me, even before I knew why. Then the marriage . . . . Ahh, Kelly." He touched her cheek with an unsteady hand. "I loved you so much, I wanted desperately to keep you with me any way I could. But not with another pregnancy, not so soon, not before . . ."

"But, Jake, I want your babies," Kelly insisted.

"And I want yours." He held her closer, smoothing kisses on her forehead. "But not for a while, please. I'd like some time to enjoy my daughter. Most of all, I want to have a wife to myself. But you must remember, Kelly, no matter how many children we have, Nicki will always be special. If it hadn't been for her, I might never have found you."

"Oh, I'm glad you found me!" she declared fiercely as she nestled into the silkiness of his throat. She was quiet for a while, then spoke drowsily, as much to herself as to him. "I know it sounds silly, you can't miss what you've never had, but I've missed being in your arms. Do you know that I dreamed almost every night that you held me while I slept?"

"It was no dream, Kelly. I did hold you. It was the little I could have and I took it with no apologies. You lay next to my heart every night."

"Jake?" She whispered his name again, loving the sound of it.

"Hmmm?"

"I love you."

"Not as much as I love you, but you can keep trying." The wicked grin of a mischievous boy lifted one corner of his mouth. "Now, how about that breakfast you promised me?"

"I'll make you the omelet," she said, but made no move to leave his embrace.

"Silly child," he scolded. "That's lunch. Any good wife knows that breakfast comes first."

Then gently and with exquisite care, he began to fold back the towel from her body.

Evening crept into a world where time had no meaning as loving, touching and loving again, they murmured drowsy nonsense.

"Now, lovely lady, about that freedom of yours."

"You're my freedom, you always were. I was setting you free."

"Just try it!"

As evening became night, Kelly stirred in Jake's arms, her head pillowed on his chest.

"Jake?" She shivered in sensual delight as his hand absently caressed the soft yielding flesh of her breasts.

"Hmm?"

"Would it really upset you if we had another baby soon?"

"Why?" His hand stilled, resting lightly, but possessively.

"Well, darling, you must admit that we haven't exactly, ah, practiced common sense." Kelly smiled softly, not displeased that she might, even now, be carrying Jake's child.

"Oh my God!" Silence. Then the first deep rumblings of a chuckle that grew to exultant laughter as it blended with hers.

"Do you see now how much I love you, Kelly?"

"Show me again."

THE EDITOR'S CORNER

With the Olympic Games in Los Angeles much on our minds these past days, we remembered a letter we got last year from Barbara York of Houston, Texas. Barbara gave us a compliment that was truly heart-warming. "If there were an Olympics for category romances," she wrote, "LOVESWEPT would win all the gold medals!"

I don't know about winning them *all* (we're always impressed by the works of talented writers in our competitors' lines). I do know, though, that all our LOVESWEPT authors and staff strive constantly for excellence in our romance publishing program . . . and that we love our work!

And now to the "solid gold" LOVESWEPTS you can expect from us next month.

Joan J. Domning is back with a marvelously evocative romance, **LAHTI'S APPLE,** LOVESWEPT #63. How this romance appeals to the senses. Place, time, sight, sound, tender emotion leap from the pages in this sensitive, yet passionate story of the growing love between heroine Laurian Bryant and hero Keska Lahti. A disillusioned musician, Keska has started an apple orchard and Laurian moves into his world to bring him fully alive. The fragrance of an apple orchard through its seasons . . . the poignant, sometimes melancholy strains of violin and cello are delightfully interwoven with delicate strands of tension between two unforgettable lovers. **LAHTI'S APPLE** stays with you, haunts like a lovely melody.

And what a treat is in store for you in Joan Bramsch's second romance, **A KISS TO MAKE IT BETTER,** LOVESWEPT #64. There's playfulness, joy, humor in

(continued)

this charming love story of Jenny Larsen, a former nurse, and Dr. Jon McCallem. But there is another dimension to this romance—the healing power of love for two sensitive human beings hurt by life's inequities. A simply beautiful story!

Billie Green appeared at one of our teas for LOVE-SWEPT readers not long ago. A lady in the audience got up during the question and answer period with authors and said, "Billie, I love your autobiographical sketches in your books almost as much as I love the books themselves. All I've got to say is thank God for your mother!" There was a big, spontaneous round of applause. Well, that "tetched" quality Billie credits her mother with having passed on to her is present with all its whimsical and enriching power in **THE LAST HERO,** LOVESWEPT #65. Billie's heroine, Toby Baxter, is funny ... but she's also so fragile a personality that you'll find yourself moist of eye and holding your breath. Then Jake Hammond, a dream of a hero—tender, powerful, yet with supreme control—begins to take gentle charge of Toby's life ... to exorcise her demons. Different, dramatic, **THE LAST HERO** is a remarkable love story.

IN A CLASS BY ITSELF, LOVESWEPT #66, by Sandra Brown is aptly titled. It *is* an absolutely spellbinding, one-of-a-kind love story. Dani Quinn is one of Sandra's most lovable heroines ever. And Logan Webster has got to be the most devastatingly attractive man Sandra's ever dreamed up. That walk, that walk, that fabulous walk of Logan's. I guarantee you'll never forget it—nor any of the other elements in this breathtakingly emotional, totally sensual romance. In my judgment, **IN A CLASS BY ITSELF** is Sandra Brown's most delicious, heartwarming love story—in short, my favorite of all her books. You won't want to miss it!

You know, these four LOVESWEPTS *do* have the properties of real gold—shine and brilliance on the surface, the true and "forever" value beneath.

Hope you agree.

Warm regards,

Carolyn Nichols

Carolyn Nichols
   Editor
LOVESWEPT
Bantam Books, Inc.
666 Fifth Avenue
New York, NY 10103

WILD SWAN

Celeste De Blasis

Author of THE PROUD BREED

Spanning decades and sweeping from England's West Country in the years of the Napoleonic Wars to the beauty of Maryland's horse country—a golden land shadowed by slavery and soon to be ravaged by war—here is a novel richly spun of authentically detailed history and sumptuous romance, a rewarding woman's story in the grand tradition of A WOMAN OF SUBSTANCE. WILD SWAN is the story of Alexandria Thaine, youngest and unwanted child of a bitter mother and distant father— suddenly summoned home to care for her dead sister's children. Alexandria—for whom the brief joys of child-hood are swiftly forgotten . . . and the bright fire of passion nearly extinguished.

Buy WILD SWAN, on sale in hardcover August 15, 1984, wherever Bantam Books are sold, or use the handy coupon below for ordering:

LOVESWEPT

*Love Stories you'll never forget
by authors you'll always remember*

☐	21603	**Heaven's Price** #1 Sandra Brown	$1.95
☐	21604	**Surrender** #2 Helen Mittermeyer	$1.95
☐	21600	**The Joining Stone** #3 Noelle Berry McCue	$1.95
☐	21601	**Silver Miracles** #4 Fayrene Preston	$1.95
☐	21605	**Matching Wits** #5 Carla Neggers	$1.95
☐	21606	**A Love for All Time** #6 Dorothy Garlock	$1.95
☐	21607	**A Tryst With Mr. Lincoln?** #7 Billie Green	$1.95
☐	21602	**Temptation's Sting** #8 Helen Conrad	$1.95
☐	21608	**December 32nd . . . And Always** #9 Marie Michael	$1.95
☐	21609	**Hard Drivin' Man** #10 Nancy Carlson	$1.95
☐	21610	**Beloved Intruder** #11 Noelle Berry McCue	$1.95
☐	21611	**Hunter's Payne** #12 Joan J. Domning	$1.95
☐	21618	**Tiger Lady** #13 Joan Domning	$1.95
☐	21613	**Stormy Vows** #14 Iris Johansen	$1.95
☐	21614	**Brief Delight** #15 Helen Mittermeyer	$1.95
☐	21616	**A Very Reluctant Knight** #16 Billie Green	$1.95
☐	21617	**Tempest at Sea** #17 Iris Johansen	$1.95
☐	21619	**Autumn Flames** #18 Sara Orwig	$1.95
☐	21620	**Pfarr Lake Affair** #19 Joan Domning	$1.95
☐	21621	**Heart on a String** #20 Carla Neggars	$1.95
☐	21622	**The Seduction of Jason** #21 Fayrene Preston	$1.95
☐	21623	**Breakfast In Bed** #22 Sandra Brown	$1.95
☐	21624	**Taking Savannah** #23 Becky Combs	$1.95
☐	21625	**The Reluctant Lark** #24 Iris Johansen	$1.95

Prices and availability subject to change without notice.

LOVESWEPT

*Love Stories you'll never forget
by authors you'll always remember*